The Long Way Home

Sanne Wijker

2012 Sveko Books

Cover design and layout Kors Wijker

Sveko books

ISBN 978-90-819613-0-1

The Long Way Home

Just a fantasy story, written for entertainment only.

Any similarity to real individuals or events is purely accidental in nature.

Build a fire a thousand miles away to light
My long way home
I ride a comet
My trail is long to stay
Silence is a heavy stone
I fight the world and take all they can give
There are times my heart hangs low
Born to walk against the wind
Born to hear my name
No matter where I stand I'm alone

Manowar, Heart of Steel.

Table of Contents

Part 1
Aargh

Part II
Delta

Part III

Tarna

Part I
AARGH

Chapter 1. Two Friends

"And still I don't get it. Why would a man of your position in society choose to become a soldier of fortune? After all, you are a lord's son." Brian looked at his friend with sincere curiosity.

Lennart laughed, showing his white teeth.

"The youngest son," he said. "Don't you know it's our tradition? The youngest son goes into the wide world to make his fortune."

"A fine way to make one's fortune, to be sure," said Brian looking around. The picture in front of him was hardly inspirational, the skies were gray with dark clouds, and a cold wind was blowing through the streets of Drianon, the capital of the planet with a long name generally known to the inhabitants of the Galactical sector X as A 364.

A long line of people was standing in front of a rather ugly building of the space haven, waiting for their turn to enter a ship which would take them back to their home planets. After the full financial meltdown following years of reckless politicies of borrowing and spending the government of A 364 had no other choice but to ask its powerful neighbor and chief creditor, Uranius to help stabilize the situation and prevent a looming civil war.

In doing so they essentially surrendered their independence as A 364 came de facto under the military rule of Uranius. Part of the stabilization pact was the deportation of a sizable minority of foreigners who had come to settle on A 364 in its more prosperous days. And the two young officers, Lennart Duncan and his friend Brian Alistair, got an honorable job of overseeing the deportation.

Both were officers in the army of the Republic of Aargh, but Aargheans were not above lending their troops to others, especially if those others offered good money. So far they had spent three months on Aargh, and those were the most boring months in Lennart's life or so he thought. He could cope with boredom rather well, but his friend Brian couldn't get to terms with the fact that he was now for all purposes in the service of

Uranius, which occupied his native Tarna and ruled it with an iron hand. He was quite bitter about the whole thing.

Lennart wasn't especially fond of Uranius, either. Uranius was one of the chief players of Sector X and the eternal rival of Delta, Lennart's home planet, so he wasn't thrilled to enforce the occupation of yet another planet, but he looked at such things philosophically. There was after all little he could do about the situation, as he had signed a contract for five years. There was still one year to go and Lennart was looking eagerly for the day when he would be his own boss. Until that blessed moment, however, there was nothing to do but to enforce the orders of his superiors, and he was doing it to the best of his abilities. He didn't react to Brian's sarcastic comment, just smiled again.

"I can call myself fortunate," he answered. "After all, I survived two wars in the mines."

"You know what I mean," said Brian. "Don't tell me you joined the army with the intention of getting rich."

"As a matter of fact, I didn't," said Lennart. "When I first came to Aargh, I found a job in construction."

Brian made some calculations in his mind and looked at his friend with doubt.

"The only big construction project seven years ago was Arshan Dam, you don't want to tell me —."

"Yes, that's where yours truly started his career," answered Lennart.

"Good God, it's little better than slavery," said Brian. "Working sixteen hours a day and all that. Was there nothing better to do?"

"Fourteen hours a day, ten on Saturday and Sunday free, and it was more free time than I knew how to use. They paid decent wages as well. What do you suppose I should have done otherwise?" Lennart could look very arrogant when he chose to.

"You don't think *I* would go into slave trade or smuggling or some such thing?"

Brian didn't have time to answer as at that moment some commotion arose in the line of waiting people. Apparently there was a quarrel between two families for the sequence. Lennart nodded to two of his soldiers waiting respectfully a couple of steps aside to follow him and hurried to the place of incident. His orders were clear, to do everything to prevent general unrest which could lead to riots.

"Get back in line." He was speaking Westen, a common language generally used in Sector X. The family consisted of two rather shabbily dressed adults, and their two teenage children, a boy and a girl. The mother was shouting something in the language Lennart could not understand and gesticulating wildly. The man tried to calm her down, but in vain. She was pointing fingers to another woman, fat and some years her senior and it looked as if the two were going to scratch each other's eyes out. Behind the fat woman a rather unpleasant looking male was making threatening gestures.

"I said, get back in line." This time, there was a sharp metallic tone in Lennart's voice. "All of you. Now." He looked at the soldiers and by his signal they raised their weapons. That produced an impression, as both sides backed down.

"That's better," said Lennart, and added addressing men: "You should control your womenfolk if you wish to leave this planet safe and sound." He went back to the place where Brian was standing with his soldiers behind him, ready to come to his friend's assistance.

"You wouldn't open fire at peaceful citizens," said Brian.

"Why shouldn't I?" asked Lennart coldly. "Of course I would if necessary."

"It would be against your code of honor," answered his friend.

"You have a lot of nonsensical ideas," said Lennart, but Brian only waved his hand.

"I know you better than you know yourself," he remarked. "Anyway, you haven't finished your story. What induced you to go to Aargh and join the army? Me, I had a price on my head after taking part in the rebellion of the year 'sixteen and no money and no idea what to do. But why did you leave your father's house?"

"Here you go again," said Lennart. "Curiosity killed the cat. I had good reasons to leave my father's house but they are my business and nobody else's. I can tell you how I joined the army though. I killed a man."

The expression on Brian's face was priceless. He was an inquisitive person and after telling his own life story to all his friends a dozen times he naturally expected confidences in return. Lennart, however, was not a talkative kind and never revealed much about himself. He didn't talk even when drunk, unlike many others, and avoided giving serious answers to any questions. Brian always suspected that there was a good reason to compel a young aristocrat to exchange his carefree existence on his native Delta for the hardships of the military life on Aargh, a planet not exactly known for its civilized way of life. Now, finally, he would learn at least something about his friend's mysterious past.

Lennart understood what was going on in his friend's mind and enjoyed the impression produced by his words. "It was in self-defence," he added, "so you don't need to make such a face. You see, as I have told you, I got Saturday evenings free and so I used to frequent a certain tavern, a very disreputable place, which naturally served superb wine and the dancing girls there..." Here Lennart paused apparently remembering what those girls were like.

"Anyway," he continued, "one day I was just sitting there in the corner minding my own business when a fight broke out, three against one. I know I shouldn't have interfered but that one was a young sickly looking fellow who was evidently a newcomer and when he fell to the ground they continued to kick him viciously and I believe they would have killed him had I not stopped them."

Lennart's light blue eyes became darker for a moment, then after a short pause he went on: "At first, I asked them politely to stop, and that caused them to leave the poor guy alone and concentrate their attention on me, but I wasn't an easy target, as they discovered, so one of them drew his gun and shot at me, but missed. I had no other choice but to draw mine in self-defence. I didn't intend to kill him, but there was little time to take aim properly, accidentaly I hit some major artery and the poor bastard died within minutes from loss of blood. The two others fled the place leaving me with a corpse on my hands. Can you imagine how I felt? He was a citizen of Aargh while I was a foreigner and should his family choose to take their complaint to court my fate would be sealed. In addition, I was informed that his friends had sworn to kill me. What was I to do? I had to disappear quickly but how? The havens were a no-go zone for me as they would be waiting for me over there. And in that dark moment the recruiter came along, promising me both the moons and all the stars of Heaven, and that's how I became a soldier of the glorious Republic of Aargh.

The rest you know. After the first war in the mines of Doran I was offered a contract as an officer and in the moment of reduced consciousness I signed it, hoping to become a general one day. So here I am now, a first lieutenant in the service of the Republic," finished Lennart.

"What a story," said Brian. He was accustomed to his friend's manner of speaking. Lennart seemed determined not to take anything or anyone seriously, not even himself.

"But as for this construction business, I thought that the contract once signed cannot be broken unless by injury or death, under the penalty of slavery."

"It can't," agreed Lennart, "but for the service in the army. All sins are forgiven to the convicted."

"So how did it all end?" asked Brian curiously. Lennart shrugged his shoulders.

"The five years during which the complaint could be filed have long passed, and recently an old acquaintance informed me that both my adversaries are dead. One got his skull broken during a bar fight, the other was murdered in the Havens. He had been involved in a drug war or something of the kind. That's how it comes that now I can tell this story even to you."

Brian got rather angry at this hint about his loose tongue but before he could think of a fitting answer he saw a figure in a military uniform approaching them and recognized Captain Ashley, their commanding officer.

Chapter 2. Captain Ashley

Captain Ashley was known for his nasty attitudes. He had sadistic inclinations and took pleasure in humiliating his inferiors, knowing that they wouldn't dare to answer him back as he deserved. Everybody hated him, even their colonel, and he had been passed over for the next promotion which naturally made his character even worse.

He disliked both Brian and Lennart and showed it whenever he got such an opportunity. This time they had to listen to a humiliating lecture given in an insulting manner about them neglecting their duties and all this in the presence of the soldiers under their command. Brian, who was hot-tempered got red in the face and had visible difficulty in controlling himself. Lennart listened with his usual ironical smile. He hated Ashley just as much as anyone else did, but he wasn't in the habit of betraying his emotions.

Of the two, Brian was an easy target, which in Lennart's opinion only encouraged the captain to pick on him more often. Lennart, on the other hand, was known for his sharp tongue, and now and then made a seemingly innocent remark in the canteen concerning the captain, which would set everyone laughing. As a result, Ashley chiefly avoided him, but doubled his attacks on Lennart's unfortunate friend.

"You shouldn't react in this manner," said Lennart the next day, when the two got the chance to talk again. They were both off duty and sitting in the "Boar", the tavern which served as a meeting place for Aarghean officers; though in Lennart's opinion it was decidedly beneath similar enterprises on Aargh. Still, the wine was decent, the waitresses rather pretty and they got a new dancing girl, a long-legged brunette of eighteen by the name of Tara, with whom Lennart hoped to get more closely acquainted in the near future.

"I propose a toast," he continued, raising his glass. "For you and me and that the devil may take Ashley."

Brian didn't seem amused.

"The bloody bastard always picks on me, always! I'll...I'll challenge him to a duel."

"He is very good with the sword, I heard," remarked Lennart, sipping his wine.

"Then you challenge him, Len," retorted Brian stubbornly. "He insulted you as well."

"A man like Captain Ashley can't insult me," said Lennart, "and besides, duels are forbidden. I'm not going to risk being court-martialed for the pleasure of humiliating him."

Brian wouldn't take "no" for an answer.

"Just remember what he called you yesterday!"

His friend shrugged his shoulders.

"I went through the Aarghean boot camp," he remarked, "during which time I was called all the names in the book. It was quite damaging for my self-esteem, but forever cured me from all delusions of grandeur."

He finished his drink and looked approvingly at Tara, who was performing her new dance. He caught her eye and the girl smiled at him. Her eyes were of a beautiful green color.

"You can think of nothing else, but girls!" exclaimed Brian, irritated. Lennart was always popular with women; they hanged on his neck and fell in love with him desperately. Lennart enjoyed the attention but never seemed to fall in love himself. He adopted an Aarghean principle according to which women existed for two purposes only, procreation and recreation, or so he said. "Love makes a warrior weak," states an Aarghean proverb, and Lennart agreed wholeheartedly, even though he was raised on Delta, where the ideas about females were more romantic.

Though he was a handsome guy, with blond hair, light blue eyes and Nordic features, not very tall but well built with well developed muscles, it was not that much his appearance that attracted girls, but rather his superior attitude.

"I do think of other things as well," he retorted. "I chiefly think about doing my duty but now I have a couple of free hours and wish to think of something else for a change."

"Oh, you are hopeless," sighed Brian. "You never can be serious, never. Think about your honor. That swine called you —."

"An idiot, I know, but I think I can live with it, while in your opinion my honor demands me to challenge him to a fight, kill him and get executed. No, thanks. I don't like the idea. I have only one year left to go and then I will be free as a bird and with money in the bank, too. I'd rather stay alive."

"Some people seem to get all the luck," said Brian unhappily. "Money always goes through my fingers, but sticks to yours somehow. And I have nearly two years to serve still."

Brian, though of the same age as Lennart, joined the army one year later. He was for some time serving under Lennart's command and that's how they got acquainted. Later he got a promotion to an officer's rank, too; and since that time, three years ago, they were friends, but he was still only a second lieutenant.

"Money sticks to me because I don't gamble," said Lennart. "Or, at least, I don't gamble when drunk and when there is no chance to win. Ever heard of such a virtue as prudence?"

"Oh, stuff it," answered Brian. "You know it's not the lack of money that upsets me. It's just that I can't cope with the fact that for all purposes I serve as a tool to enforce the Uranius's politics of aggression."

"The locals made a pretty mess out of things, what with uncontrolled immigration leading to an ethnic conflict which they did nothing to prevent, irresponsible spending and all other ill-conceived policies; at least now they'll get some semblance of order. I'm not going to lose my sleep at night because of it," replied Lennart calmly. He ordered another drink.

"I know it's different for you," said Brian, "but I practically feel myself a traitor. All my friends were hanged or got lengthy prison terms only because they dared to wish for independence, and here I am serving the enemy."

"You serve the Republic of Aargh," reminded Lennart. "And anyway there is nothing you can do about it. You signed the contract and you swore the oath of allegiance to the Republic."

"Oh no? I could always leave and go somewhere else."

At that point, Lennart got worried. He looked at his friend trying to understand if the latter was speaking seriously. Brian's dark brown eyes flashed and he was really quite agitated. Tarnians ethnically were closely related to the citizens of Delta, but Brian belonged to the southern type so he had dark eyes and dark hair, and he looked much more like a native of Aargh than his blond friend.

"Brian, you are crazy. Don't even think of it! If you desert, you will be sentenced to death and you'll never be able to appear anywhere close to Aargh without taking a huge risk. Where will you go? Back to Tarna? If I were you I'd get it out of my head. After all, it's just two more years and then you will be honorably retired, with pension, veteran benefits and all that. Besides, if you break the oath of allegiance, you really will be a traitor."

Brian wasn't at all convinced by his friend's arguments, he thought by himself that there were plenty of places he could go to if he left Aargh, but he was not in the mood to continue the discussion any further. He was in the mood to get drunk and succeeded in it before the evening was over.

Several days passed without any events, during which Lennart hardly ever saw his friend and he totally forgot about their last conversation. It was Friday evening by the standard calendar, Lennart could look forward to two days off duty that week and he finally came to an understanding with Tara. She was sitting on his lap listening to his compliments and giggling.

Some other officers were playing cards at the next table, enjoying a sweet melody in the background. At that moment the tavern door opened and a patrol of military police entered the scene.

"Lieutenant Duncan, you are arrested on a charge of treason."

Before Lennart could fully comprehend the meaning of these words, they handcuffed him and dragged away, leaving Tara behind to sob hysterically.

Chapter 3. Lennart Gets into Trouble

The next week Lennart spent in the military prison, in solitary confinement. One evening he was sitting on the dirty mattress staring at the wall in front of him in a dimly lit cell without windows and thinking what bad luck he had. Brian did desert after all, carrying away some papers which were generally referred to as TOP SECRET. If that had not been enough, he tried to shoot Captain Ashley, but (unfortunately, as Lennart thought), missed and only wounded the captain in his left arm.

The wound was not dangerous at all and did not prevent Ashley from participating in the interrogations of Lennart who had been accused of acting as his friend's accomplice. One comfort in that whole story was that Lennart finally fulfilled his dream of punching the captain on the nose; as a result of which he himself got a black eye and was kept in chains all the time.

He looked around him now and swore, but didn't feel any better. "And to think," he said to himself, "that I had less than a year left to serve. If that idiotic Brian had decided to do the dastardly captain in, he could have at least done it properly, but the only thing that he achieved is that Ashley is now visiting all his frustrations upon my head."

Lennart's reflections were of a sober kind. Ashley, a native of Aargh, had some highly connected relatives. He never could stand Lennart, and finally got his chance to revenge. Lennart was sick of being interrogated three times a day, wondered if they would go third degree on him, and dreaded to think about how the whole story would end if they didn't believe him.

There was no proof that he had anything to do with Brian's plans at all, but he had been Alistair's best friend for three years, everybody knew it, and in these types of situations they often just want to find anyone they can pronounce guilty and make an example of.

When his thoughts reached that point, Lennart started feeling profoundly miserable. He rose and began walking to and fro, muttering, "Why won't they believe me?" but the cell was small and didn't give him much space for excercise.

Finally he got tired, lay down upon his mattress and fell asleep, and immediately got a nightmare in which Captain Ashley and Colonel Higgs used electroshock on him, while he was screaming: "I don't know anything! Leave me alone!"

In reality, Higgs was sitting in his office. He looked at the clock, then at the pile of papers on his desk and sighed. It was getting late and he still didn't have time for dinner, only coffee. He called his secretary and asked for another cup, then told him to let in Captain Ashley and Major Grant who was in charge of the investigation. Both were waiting in the reception room.

Higgs was in his mid-forties, still a well-looking man, half Aarghean half Deltan by blood. He was sympathetic with his lieutenant and he disliked Ashley profoundly.

"I don't believe Duncan is guilty," he said. "There is not a shred of evidence against him, or am I wrong, Major?"

"No, sir," replied Grant. "Outside of the fact that he had been friends with Alistair."

"It doesn't prove anything," said Higgs. "Alistair had a lot of friends, must we arrest them all? If Duncan is guilty, why did he stay behind? Couldn't he have figured out that he would be the first suspect? I think we should release Lieutenant Duncan from custody."

"What, will he not be punished at all?" asked Captain Ashley angrily. "He broke my nose."

"You shouldn't have taunted him, Captain," said Higgs unsympathetically. "Lieutenant Duncan is a war veteran; he was twice wounded and has a silver cross and the star of hero for the operation "No Escape". Naturally, he didn't like being called a traitor."

"It was still insubordination, at the very least," insisted Ashley.

"It still doesn't give us a reason to court-martial him for espionage and high treason," remarked the colonel. "Well, what do you think, Major?"

"I agree, sir,"said Grant. "After the thorough investigation the comission came to the conclusion that Lieutenant Duncan had nothing to do with the whole story."

"They found out it was likely a Deltan agent who had given the task of stealing the documents to Alistair," said Ashley. "Doesn't it prove anything? After all, Duncan himself is a Deltan!"

"My mother was a Deltan as well," retorted Higgs. "Does this fact make me guilty of treason?" Ashley became very red and shut his mouth.

"Enough arguing," said Higgs. "I think we'd better release Lieutenant Duncan and the sooner the better. On the other hand, I also think it will be wise to transfer him back to Aargh."

"The transport is leaving tomorrow, sir," said Major Grant. "At midday."

"Fine," smiled Higgs, "tomorrow at nine we will announce him our decision. It will give him nearly three hours to pack his things. And now, gentlemen, I want to wish you a very good evening."

The next morning Lennart was as usual contemplating his misfortunes. He just finished his breakfast which had consisted of something distantly reminding a crescent roll and a cup of very inferiorly tasting coffee. At that moment the heavy door of his cell opened and he saw four guards and a young lieutenant Higgs who was a nephew to the colonel and bore the same name.

Lennart thought of another tiresome interrogation and sighed, but there was nothing to do but to follow the guards. Higgs smiled at him as if he wanted to cheer him up but didn't say anything outside of polite formalities. Lennart was ushered into the colonel's office and saw Higgs senior, Ashley, Grant and the two other members of the investigation comission. Lennart stood in the entrance looking at them and they looked back at him and their faces were serious.

Finally after what seemed a very long pause, Higgs spoke: "Lieutenant Duncan, the comission in charge of the investigation did not find any evidence of your participation in the Alistair espionage affair. You are thus cleared of the accusations of treason, espionage and being an accessory to a first degree murder attempt."

He ordered the guards to remove the handcuffs and continued while Lennart was rubbing his wrists. "You will be transferred to Aargh, your transport leaves in about three hours. Before you go, I want that unfortunate business with Captain Ashley to be settled. Here, shake each other's hands. It's not becoming to the fellow officers to hold grudges against one another."

Lennart did as he had been told, noting with satisfaction black circles under the captain's eyes and the form of his nose. "Hopefully he'll need a surgery to fix it", he thought and then remembered that he had less than three hours left to pack. There was no time to say good-bye to Tara.

Chapter 4. The Planet of Aargh

Aargh was a large planet, the largest in Sector X. It had two moons, and its year was equal to two standard years (standard calendar based on that used on Delta and similar to the one used on Earth in our times). The climate of Aargh was mostly tropical; though it had a couple of deserts, a large part of the planet was covered by rain forests and jungles, cut by mountains with peaks well above 10.000 meters. There were two principal seasons, the rain season and the dry season.

The Republic of Aargh controlled the largest part of the planet territory, and its capital bore the same name as the planet itself: Aargh. The city of Aargh was situated in the middle of a great plateau and had a dry and sunny climate, with only a moderate amount of rain.

Aargh was a strange, fascinating place, truly the world full of contrasts: between poverty and riches, slums and gated communities, freedom and slavery. It was a place where one could quickly become insanely rich or dirt poor, home for the adventure seekers from the whole universe, a safe haven for smugglers and the chief slave trade centre of the galaxy.

It wasn't a secret to anyone that three things made the Republic rich: slave trade, weapons trade and diamond trade. Slavery was prohibited on most planets of the galaxy. The rich and liberal Galactical Trade Federation constantly complained about its existence in Sector X. Pious politicians on Delta made TV speeches about the necessity of its eradication, but nobody wanted to start a major war.

The Republic of Aargh was politically neutral, but it maintained a strong army, using an old principle: If you wish for peace, be prepared for war. Defense was the principal point in the Republic's budget. It had no welfare, except for disabled military veterans who got free medical treatment, ample pensions and other benefits.

The society of Aargh was strongly class divided, the chief distinction being between slave or free, and between citizens and non-citizens. Aargh was an immigration planet but it never had any troubles with immigrants, unlike others who tried the same policy. Non-citizens on Aargh had no political rights and no representation. Unless they were rich foreigners who came in for business, they were left totally to fend for themselves. Police seldom visited the slums where they lived.

The justice system on Aargh was rather simple. The state only prosecuted the crimes against the state itself, such as espionage or high treason. The crimes against private citizens were the family business, the family could choose to file a complaint or not, and it had to be done within a certain time, the longest being for murder— five years. After that time passed there was no manner to get a legal redress.

The punishments were harsh, and chiefly consisted of death, being sold into slavery or public whipping. A non-citizen had very little chance of winning any court case against a citizen, and slaves had none. It's logical to conclude that most immigrants wanted to get a citizen status as it conferred many privileges.

There were two ways to do it: one could buy it, but he had first to be extremely rich, or one could get it by serving a minimum of three years as a soldier of the Republic. The latter was by no means a safe way, as the army was regularly used to solve domestic problems on the planet itself and hired out for money for the military operations on other planets.

The mortality rate was high; and Lennart was right to consider himself lucky as he was the only person of his initial company who had survived the first Doran war. Further on, Aargheans had certain preferences when recruiting new soldiers; they prefered those closely related to them and sharing some common concepts, such as Deltans, Tarnians, Uranians or the natives of the Baron Confederation to the inhabitants of Volcan and similar planets. Officers were chiefly of Aarghean origin, though exceptions were made for those soldiers who had shown themselves capable.

The only way to get the citizenship for a woman was to marry an Aarghean. Children of an Aarghean father born within wedlock were automatically considered citizens, but the citizenship was never conferred in a female line.

This was the world which Lennart saw for the first time when he was eighteen and like many others before him, he was strongly fascinated by it. It had its own charm and was cruel and beautiful at the same time, intoxicating and exotic. Human life had little value there, and the law of the jungle was the rule of the slums.

On Aargh, there were few laws protecting workers' rights and none protecting the rights of the foreign employees, outside of the laws barring foreigners from certain and women from nearly all professions with the exception made for domestic servants, dancing girls, waitresses and prostitutes.

Strange enough, though Aargh hosted the biggest annual slave market of the galaxy, it was considered a low class behavior to have slaves, and the upper classes of the Republic generally had none.

Like nearly all the planets of Sector X, the rulers of Aargh were concerned with modern conveniences making life too easy and the citizens too soft;

and automatization taking away jobs from men, so a lot of modern devices designed to make life easier, such as various robots, were prohibited (this prohibition extending to military robots and drones), just like on Delta and Uranius; which gave even more grounds for the representatives of the Galactical Trade Federation to dismiss them as barbarians.

Lennart had missed Aargh, he also got accustomed to a warm climate; and had difficulty with adapting to the weather on A364, which for the most part of his stay there was chilly, gloomy and wet. Thus he was happy to come back, even happier still because he was finally rid of captain Ashley, but he missed Brian's company even though he was angry with his friend for having deserted in such a manner, leaving him to face the consequences.

Sometimes he wondered where Brian was and whether they'd see each other again. There was little chance for it, he thought, as long as he himself stayed on Aargh, unless his friend had suicidal inclinations. Brian had been sentenced to death in absentia, and it would be highly unwise for him to venture to show himself anywhere in the proximity of the planet any time soon.

Chapter 5. Operation "Dawn of Hope"

It was the end of the rain season and the end of the standard year '22 when the operation "Dawn of Hope" started. As it had been mentioned before, the Republic of Aargh controlled a large part of the territory of the planet, but by no means all of it. There were other states, most of them loyal to the Republic, some of them not.

The last years the Republic was expanding and it seemed as if it decided not to tolerate any rivals any more. The latest confrontation was Doran wars, which were fought for the control of a mountain area rich in precious metals. The government of the area had refused to pay the tax demanded by Aargh, and this led to an armed conflict which lasted in total six years and caused a huge loss of human life.

The Republic emerged victorious and more prosperous than ever, now that it had all the revenues of the sale of those metals, as for human life, since most of the soldiers who had fought and died were foreigners, nobody on Aargh was especially concerned about their fate. War reduced the amount of young immigrant males who could otherwise cause trouble, and in the opinion of the rulers of the Republic, it was a necessary thing now and then.

The operation "Dawn of Hope" was, however, a slightly different affair. Several thousand kilometers away from the capital, on the coast of an ocean there was a rich city called Sant Aargh, which in name acknowledged the supremacy of the Republic of Aargh, but de facto was left to its own devices. Sant Aargh and the area around it, consisting of jungles and a mountain chain by the name of Azida were from time immemorial an asylum for pirates, outlaws and all sorts of unsavory characters which even the Republic of Aargh would not tolerate.

Aargh was a planet with vast natural resources and that part of it wasn't an exception; as there were precious stones in the mountains of Azida. The exploitation of the mines, the profits from the slave trade and the income from piracy and smuggling were the things which made Sant Aargh rich.

There was little industry there and machinery and weapons had to be imported. The inhabitants of Sant Aargh paid a small tribute to the Republic, but they were chiefly tolerated because they were far away, and war with them was deemed too expensive. However, the main reason of this tolerance was probably the fact that the pirates living there made some important galactical trade routes unsafe, thus undermining the economy of other planets which was in direct interests of Aargh, whose rulers did not desire that their neighbors would become too prosperous.

There were other forces which wished to use the pirates in their own interests, and more or less succeeded. The last couple of years trade ships of Delta and the Baron Confederation had been repeatedly attacked and it wasn't a secret to anyone who was the instigator of those attacks. Uranius, the eternal rival of Delta, the planet always trying to expand its power used pirates of Sant Aargh as proxy in their never ending cold war with their adversary.

For some time Deltans were content with hunting down and destroying the pirate ships in the open space, but it didn't stop the attacks. Supplied with money and weapons by Uranians, the pirates only became more insolent, and finally the patience of Delta reached its limit. The new government was elected on the promises of eradicating the evil of piracy forever and curbing the appetites of Uranius.

They started with more or less an ultimatum to the government of the Republic of Aargh: either the latter would help them by undertaking a local military action against the coastal areas under the control of the pirates, or the Deltan fleet would strike from the orbit burning the pirate city to the ground and destroying the whole area in the process.

The Aarghean rulers thought it over. The strike from space would destroy everything and make the area unsuitable to live in for years to come. They could choose to see it as an act of aggression and retaliate, but it would mean a full scale war with powerful Delta which in all probability would be backed by the Barons as well; on the other hand, if they cooperated they would gain control of the whole territory and the mines. Also, the Republic was not thrilled with the growing influence of Uranius and its trying to get a hold on the territory of the planet.

And so it happened that having considered the issue the government of Aargh took the decision to start the military operation which came to be known as "Dawn of Hope".

The plan of the operation was simple. The combined forces of Delta and the Republic would blockade the havens of the pirates from space thus depriving them of necessary supplies while Aargheans would also undertake air strikes and a ground operation. The authorities of Aargh hoped that small scale interference would be enough to force the pirates to surrender, as after six years of fighting in Doran they were not keen on starting another major war so soon.

Lennart coming back to Aargh anticipated a rather pleasant life in the capital with a lot of time off duty in a city where one could find entertainment easily, after all he had only several months left to serve; the war was over, his contract would expire soon too, those were all pleasant prospects. He didn't take into consideration the operation "Dawn Of Hope" and the fact that though he had been acquitted he was still on the list of suspicious characters, and thus the first candidate to be sent into some dangerous enterprise.

Before a month passed since his return to Aargh he was deployed to Istar, the capital of the area called Varya bordering on Azida which was controlled by Aargh, and where the Republic had numerous military bases which were to be used for the anti-pirate action. When he was promoted to an officer rank, Lennart had to learn how to pilot a craft, though he wasn't really good at it. Now he had to undergo a remedial two month course after which he was raised in rank to captain and sent to fly missions over Azida and Sant Aargh.

Chapter 6. Shot Down over Azida

If the objective of those who had decided Lennart should take part in the operation "Dawn of Hope" was to get rid of him quickly and without any effort on their part, they were disappointed in their plans as Lennart managed to keep himself alive for three subsequent months despite his inferior skills as a pilot, while his more skilled comrades died one after another.

The small scale operation proved to be bloodier than anyone had expected as the pirates fought desperately, knowing they would probably receive no quarter in case they lost. They used guerilla war tactics with small isolated groups attacking the villages of Varya, blowing up bridges, taking hostages and exploding bombs at the markets.

They did not have enough fighter crafts to intercept those of the Aargheans, but they had enough anti-air missiles and counter-air defence systems to make bombing missions dangerous. The pilots who managed to survive when their craft had been shot down were nearly always hunted and killed in a brutal manner.

Lennart saw his friends leave and never return, and yet he always came back, as if by a miracle. He believed in his lucky star, after all he had managed to stay alive so far, but one day his luck abandoned him when he was shot down on his way back from Sant Aargh nearly four hundred kilometers away from the base in Istar.

Lennart left the burning craft at the very last moment, and it exploded right above his head rendering him unconscious. When he came back to his senses, he was hanging in a tree, his parachute caught on one of its branches. He was feeling dizzy and it took him some time to realize what predicament he was in.

He was on the enemy territory and the enemy was probably not far away. Luckily he wasn't wounded, he thought as he was struggling to free himself. Finally he fell to the ground, but scrambled back to his feet, took off and threw away his helmet, and at this very moment, before he could even decide which direction to go, he was surrounded by pirates.

They had come from nowhere it seemed, and there was nothing he could do. They were with a group of seven men, all heavily armed and he even didn't get a chance to pull his raygun out. They searched him, took away his weapons, tied his hands behind his back and started talking to each other in their language which was a dialect of common Aarghean, but Lennart couldn't understand it very well.

He remembered all the horror stories he had heard about pirates' treatment of prisoners. Lennart had an uneasy feeling that his captors were discussing which manner to choose to send him back to his Maker, that is whether they should cut his throat, hang him or blow his brains out. The majority seemed to be for the first option. Lennart realized he had probably little time left to live. It was necessary to do something quickly, but what?

He licked his dry lips and addressed the pirates in a desperate attempt to save his life, "You shouldn't really kill me," he said. His voice was coarse, as his mouth was suddenly very dry. "Your superiors won't like it at all."

One of the pirates which was apparently the leader of the group, a man about thirty five years old, unshaved, with long dark hair gathered in a pony tail and a knife scar upon his face came close to him. He had a dagger in his hand. "And why is this?" he asked, speaking common Aarghean with a strange nasal accent.

"Because I have some important information, which your commanders will like to know," lied Lennart. He didn't know anything of any importance but there was no time to invent a more credible story.

"You tell it to me and I will decide whether it's important or not," said the pirate.

"It's about a new operation," said Lennart. "Take me to your commander, he should hear first about those things. He won't appreciate it if I tell you before he knows."

"How can I be sure you are not lying?" asked the pirate suspiciously.

"I am not," insisted Lennart. "Anyway, let your commander decide."

The pirate seemed to be hesitating and Lennart saw his chance so he continued: "Of course, you can kill me now, but you'll come to regret it. Your superiors won't like it at all. You'll get no promotion.You —."

"Shut up," said the pirate, hitting him across his face. "I'll take you to our field commander; let him decide what to do with you. But if you are lying you'll regret the day you were born."

Lennart had to follow the pirates which was difficult to do with his hands tied behind his back so that he stumbled and fell numerous times to the entertainment of his captors. If he had thought he'd have an opportunity to escape on the way to the pirate camp, he was sorely mistaken as there was not the slightest chance to do it. He tried to think of what he was going to say, but he felt too much confused and dizzy. The situation seemed to be totally hopeless.

Finally they reached their destination, which was not that far off, it took them less than an hour to get there, and for Lennart the time seemed to go too quick. The pirate camp consisted of a row of tents, among which armed men were walking. They all looked alike, with their dark beards and dark green uniforms without any signs of distinction.

There were some women in the camp, too, who were evidently slaves, judging by their clothes. Free women on Aargh always wore black cloaks; their dresses normally fell all the way to the ground and they usually covered their hair with black scarves. The women in the camp were bare-headed, their dresses were so short that they hardly covered the knees, but they were relatively young and pretty. They stopped whatever they were doing and stared at the prisoner until the men chased them away.

One tent stood apart and it was evidently the commander's. It was guarded by two young pirates with heavy rifles. Lennart was brought to it and had to wait while the group leader was talking to the guards and some other pirates who had joined them. All were gesticulating wildly and pointing to the prisoner, Lennart tried to understand what they were saying but in vain. They were talking too quickly and he was dizzy, tired and could barely stand upon his feet.

One of the guards went inside, then returned and Lennart was pushed unmercifully in his back so that he nearly fell.

"Forward, you swine," said the pirate with the scar. "Now you'll get a chance to tell your story to the commander."

Lennart was brought inside the tent, which was quite spacious and not devoid of comfort, but he didn't look around. He had eyes only for the man who was sitting on a chair in front of a small portable desk. He had been apparently eating as in front of him there lay an unfinished sandwich and he had a cup of coffee in his hand which he put down and looked at Lennart. Their eyes met.

For a long moment Lennart stared at the person before him and then the exclamation of surprise escaped his lips, for the field commander of the pirates was nobody else but Brian Alistair!

Chapter 7. In The Pirate Camp

Brian rose upon his feet and said something and as a result the ropes tying Lennart's hands were cut. He approached his friend and exclaimed: "I still can't believe my eyes! Could it really be you? What a strange coincidence!"

"I can't believe my eyes, either," replied Lennart, whose vision had been rather blurred, "but I can believe my ears, I guess. Since it definitely is Brian's voice you must be him or him must be you. Which reminds me that there is one thing I desperately wanted to do all these months."

He took a step back and punched his friend in the face with all the strength he could gather. Brian fell to the ground; the pirates shouted and jumped at Lennart grabbing him by his arms. He felt a knife blade upon his throat. Brian struggled back to his feet and swore. "Let him go," he shouted and added something incomprehensible. The knife was taken away, the pirates drew back reluctantly and left the tent.

"Why the hell did you do it?" asked Brian reproachfully. "You really haven't changed much in this half a year, Len."

"Because it was a pretty rotten trick to play," said Lennart. "Disappearing like this without saying good-bye and leaving me with the consequences, not to mention having to deal with Ashley."

"Ashley? Is he not dead then?" asked Brian surprised.

"You could never shoot straight," said Lennart.

"But I saw him fall to the ground!"

"He was wounded," explained Lennart, "but when he came back to his senses, guess who did he blame for his ordeal? He stated that I was the instigator. Do you comprehend what scrape I was in?"

"I had no idea they'd charge you, I swear," stated Brian solemnly. "How could I know? As for Ashley, what a pity. Was his wound dangerous?"

"He got over it," said Lennart and swayed. He had braced himself before he entered the tent to prepare for the worst, and now he finally got the reaction.

"You aren't wounded, are you?" asked Brian, worried. "I'll call the doctor. They tell me your plane was shot down."

"I don't think I am," replied Lennart. "I just feel dizzy, that's all. It must be because of that explosion."

"Just lie down," said Brian showing him the improvised bed on the floor. "I'll go get the doctor."

Lennart watched his friend disappear and realized that he hadn't asked him by what strange chance he had joined the pirates. Brian soon came back accompanied by the doctor, who after a brief examination declared that there was nothing wrong with Lennart outside of a light concussion which was to be expected in these circumstances and recommended rest and quiet.

"You just need a good cup of coffee and a couple of hours of sleep, that's all," said Brian.

"First you have to tell me how on Aargh did you get here," insisted Lennart. "I thought you despised the idea of collaborating with Uranius, and yet it's them who are behind the pirates."

Brian's face became gloomy. "It's a long story," he said. "I had to go to Sant Aargh after I had left A364 and so I found myself there when the war started. I tried to leave, it was before the blockade was enforced, and Sant Aargh officially rebelled. It was a free city still and not everybody agreed with pirates, but they got the upper hand in the city council. They wanted to take a resolution that every able-bodied man should be drafted, but it didn't get enough support. You see, Sant Aargh is huge and divided into spheres of influence, so that the war party didn't control it all. They let it be for some time, but would patrol the suburbs, kidnap random men and force them to join the rebel groups. I had to go outside the city once on some business and was intercepted by such a group. With a knife at my throat, what else could I do? Since I had military experience I quickly became a field commander."

Brian didn't explain why he would venture into an unsafe neighborhood and Lennart didn't ask him, though he had some suspicions.

"Well, I hope your vulgar curiosity is satisfied," finished Brian his story. "And now try to get some sleep. You'll tell me about your adventures later."

"There is not much to tell," said Lennart sleepily. "I was arrested and accused of espionage and what not. It was sheer luck and the good will of colonel Higgs which saved me from an appointment with a firing squad, I guess. Then they sent me back to Aargh just in time so that I could take part in their new war, the rest you know. By the way, it will probably give you some satisfaction to know that I broke Ashley's nose during an interrogation. He'll need surgery to fix it."

"That's some good news," laughed Brian and then he left the tent.

Lennart drank a cup of coffee they brought him and quickly fell asleep. He slept nearly the whole day and when he woke up in the evening he was feeling much better and got back his appetite. He was alone in the tent and thus had some time to think the situation over. He was wondering what Brian had told the pirates under his command. Surely they needed a credible story as to why their prisoner was set free, he thought. And what was his future? Would they let him go? Did he want to go? He'd lose the benefits and the pension, to be sure, but was there any chance he'd live as long as to collect them, taking into consideration the war?

Despite the blockade, there was still a possibility to leave Sant-Aargh, he and Brian could go somewhere else together. Did he not have enough of fighting by now? Before he could answer these questions for himself he was interrupted as Brian entered the tent carrying a flash light in his hand.

"So you are awake," he said, coming closer. "And looking much better, too. Just in time for dinner."

On the way to the canteen they both weren't very talkative, each having something to think about. The canteen was a big tent, full of pirates, some of them sitting outside as well. It was a clear night with not one cloud in the sky and both moons were shining. The dinner was good though rather simple, after it was over the women collected and washed the dishes and then the entertaiment began.

The slave girls who had been serving men, started dancing and singing. Lennart, sitting outside, watched them move graciously in the wild dance rhythm, but there was one of the girls who especially attracted his attention.

She was not older than twenty, he thought, and looked like someone who had belonged to the upper class of the Aarghean society. She had dark red-auburn hair, very white skin and a slender body and her eyes were of a deep blue color. Lennart thought her remarkably beautiful. He remembered now that she had been one of the women staring at him when he was first brought to the camp. She didn't dance though; she was still busy cleaning up after dinner.

Suddenly there was a commotion in the camp. A guard came running, he said something to Brian and the latter disappeared. Lennart wasn't feeling really comfortable. The whole evening Brian had avoided answering any questions and he wasn't sure what his position exactly was. The pirates didn't talk to him, either; they only kept staring at him in an unfriendly manner.

Brian came back and there were two men accompanying him. They both had long black beards and looked like those who were accustomed to the immediate obedience of everyone around them. Lennart could not exactly determine their age, since it was dark and the beards made every man look older, but he thought they both must be thirty at the very least.

Brian was talking rapidly, gesticulating. The three of them broke the circle of the spectators, causing dancing and singing to cease abruptly. They looked at Lennart and came close to the place where he was sitting and he knew immediately that something went wrong, terribly wrong.

“Get up,” said one of the men. “On your feet.”

Lennart did as he had been told.

“So that’s your prisoner,” said the man addressing Brian in common Aarghean. It was very quiet, as nobody else dared to speak. “A captain in the army of Aargh,” the man continued. “A pilot. One probably responsible for the death of hundreds of our men.”

At these words, there was a murmur among the pirates. “What can you say for yourself?”

“In the army one simply follows orders one gets,” answered Lennart. “I was not given a choice; I was commanded to fly those missions.”

The pirate smiled suddenly, showing all his teeth. They were yellow and one was missing. Lennart thought it was a very unpleasant smile.

“So,” said the man, “if I understand you correctly you didn’t do it out of your own free will. It changes the whole business, doesn’t it? Alistair here tells me you have a lot of experience fighting. We need men like you. So this time you will be given a choice. You can join us or you’ll die.”

At his command two pirates rose to their feet. Lennart was grabbed by his arms. He didn’t try to resist as he knew it was futile. The third pirate pulled back his head by his hair and Lennart felt cold steel on his throat.

“You had thirty seconds to think my proposal over,” said the pirate chief. “They are over by now. So what’s your answer?”

Of all the ways a man could die that one seemed particularly apalling to Lennart. He had a vivid imagination and saw himself convulsing on the ground, in a pool of his own blood. And yet, despite this, suddenly he knew the answer to the question he had asked himself earlier this day. He knew it now. He could not break the vows, given out of his own free will, to serve the Republic. Even if it meant death. Death was better than dishonor. He realized that he could not live with himself if he bought his life by such a price.

Lennart looked at the chief, took a deep breath and spoke: “No, never! I’ll never join your side! And now go on, finish me, do it quickly.”

He expected to die that very moment; there was mist in front of his eyes and a strange sound in his ears, when as if from a distance he heard a slightly familiar voice, saying: "Don't do it. We can always kill him, but I think there is a better way to deal with him than that one."

Lennart recognized the voice, it belonged to Brian. The mist became thinner. The knife was taken away.

"What do you mean?" asked the chief.

"We can earn a lot of money if we sell him as a slave," continued Brian. "Just look at him, he is in a good condition. Look at his muscles. He can work sixteen hours a day, easily. If we kill him, we get nothing."

The chief was hesitating. "Sounds like a good plan to me," he said finally.

Lennart felt as if the ground under his feet gave way and he was falling into an abyss. He had heard about the life of slaves in the mines. Death was infinitely preferable to such an existence. His self-control broke. "No, o God, no!" he cried. "Bloody bastards! Better kill me, now!"

The chief laughed. "You were right, Alistair. This will be a much better punishment for him and he seems to understand it. Death is an easy way out."

Lennart fought madly, but to no avail. They tied him by hands and feet, dragged him back to Brian's tent, threw upon the ground like a sack of potatoes and left him alone in the dark.

Chapter 8. Eileen

Lennart didn't know how much time he had spent alone in the darkness of the tent. At first he tried to free himself but the ropes were strong enough to withstand all his desperate attempts and all the knots held well. Then he was seized by a fit of despair as black as the darkness itself.

He had been beaten unmercifully and knocked on his head a couple of times. He hadn't felt any pain at first, but now he was overcome by it, his head was aching, his wrists were cut by the ropes he had been trying to get rid of. Lennart was dizzy and sick and felt as if he were slipping into a black hole. The darkness took him.

When he regained his consciousness it took him some time to realize where he was and remember what had happened. He didn't know what time it was except that it was still night. At the distance he heard some drunken voices singing a song, then everything was quiet. Suddenly Lennart heard footsteps. They were light footsteps, those of a woman. She went inside, a shadow in the darkness. He could hear her breathing, then she knelt near him.

"Keep still," she whispered. Her voice was melodic. "I'm a friend. I'm here to help you." With a swift movement she cut the ropes binding the prisoner. To say that Lennart was surprised was an understatement. His astonishment could not be greater. He sat up with difficulty and looked at the woman trying to distinguish her features in the dark.

"Why are you doing this?" he whispered. "Do you realize you are risking your life?"

"I don't want to keep on living as a slave," replied the girl. "I'd rather die as a free woman. There is no time to talk, let's get out of here, quick."

"But the guards," asked Lennart, "what about them?"

"They are all drunk," she answered with disgust. "We have a couple of hours, but we should act quickly. Here, take this."

She pushed something into his hand, and Lennart realized it was a gun. He didn't try to ask her any more questions but followed her outside. The night grew darker as one of the moons had disappeared and a fresh wind was blowing from the mountains but there was still enough light for Lennart to recognize his rescuer. It was the girl with the auburn hair he had noticed and admired several hours before. Her dress, though longer than a typical slave girl dress, was rather tight and displayed her figure well and Lennart again thought how beautiful she was.

“What’s your name?” he whispered.

“Eileen,” said the girl, “and now please, do not talk, just follow me.”

He did without asking any more questions. They went through the outskirts of the camp, leaving the central square where the big canteen tent stood, on the side. The only other living beings they came across were a couple of drunken pirates sleeping on the ground. Finally, they reached the place where the pirates kept their vehicles. Lennart looked around, but there was still no one to be seen. No guards, nothing. The girl sighed with relief.

There were six cars standing, two trucks, one to carry supplies and one to transport people, three weather-beaten four wheel drives, and one brand new 4x4 which by the look of it cost more than all the others together. An empty jerry-can stood close to it. Lennart tried the door, it was open. The keys were left in the ignition as well.

“Get in and give me the knife,” said Lennart to the slave girl and quickly proceeded to cut the fuel lines in the engines of the other five vehicles. Now they could finally leave. Eileen sat next to him and Lennart turned the ignition key and saw that just as he had expected the car had a full tank of fuel. He thought by himself that 4x4 apparently belonged to the two newcomers and that it was filled up for the trip back to where they had come from. The pirates were rather careless, but it was probably because they were sure nothing could possibly go wrong.

At that moment a very familiar voice behind him asked: “Just where do you think you are going?” Lennart turned, a raygun in his hand, ready to shoot and saw Brian rising from the back seat where he evidently had been hiding all the time.

Lennart cursed. He knew he should kill Brian so that he wouldn’t betray him again, but he couldn’t bring himself to do it so he just said: “Get out of the darned car and leave your weapons behind.” He thought by himself that it would take Brian some time to warn the pirates in any case and besides, the other cars were damaged so that they still had a chance to escape.

“Careful with this thing,” said Brian pointing to the raygun in Lennart’s hand. “It’s rather dangerous”.

“I know,” hissed Lennart through his teeth. “I’m going to count to ten. One, two —.”

“Won’t you even give me a chance for an explanation?” asked Brian reproachfully. “Have you asked yourself how it comes that the car has a full tank of fuel, the door is open and the keys are in? And no guards around. By the way, I could have killed both of you before you'd realize something was going wrong."

Lennart looked stunned. He could see his friend grinning. "You mean that —."

"Yes," nodded Brian, "I do mean that it was all my work. By the way, you didn't answer my question. Do you have any idea which way to go? I think you'd better let me drive."

"I don't trust him," said Eileen. Lennart was hesitating.

"I think you owe us an explanation," he said.

"There is no time for explanations," answered Brian impatiently. "But I know how stubborn you are so here it is: The two who brought all this trouble upon us, came unexpectedly from Sant Aargh with orders to evacuate the camp. I didn't expect them, and had no time to invent a decent story so I just told them the truth. That you were a friend of mine, and that we had served together. You'll excuse me, but I also added that you were sick of fighting in the Aarghean wars of aggression and were possibly planning to join us. What else could I say? They don't exactly like members of the Aarghean military over here. I had no time to warn you, but I thought that you'd have enough sense —."

Here Lennart interrupted him angrily. "Just because you broke your vows it doesn't mean others will as well."

"Your idealism is your problem," said Brian tiredly. "And please, let me finish my story. I told you that I didn't become a pirate out of my own free will. I was thinking about leaving and after I had met you I finally became sure it'd be a correct thing to do, but I had no time.... Anyway, when you declared you'd rather die I had to act quickly to save your life and I succeeded, though I see now that I didn't earn your gratitude. My plan was to wait till they are all drunk, as on the occasion of the visit by superiors I had ordered to give them nearly all supplies of booze we had in the camp, then to free you and to get away, but that girl," he pointed to Eileen, "apparently got the same idea and was the first to act. I pretended to be sleeping but I watched her and decided that the best thing to do would be to go to the parking place and to wait for you in the car."

"And how exactly did you know that I'd choose this one?" asked Lennart suspiciously.

"Should I say because I knew that your esthetic sense would demand choosing the best car available? Or because your common sense would choose the car with a full tank? I'd say both," finished Brian his story. "Other cars wouldn't start anyway," he added, "a little sugar goes a long way, you know. And now please, enough talking, we have lost a lot of time already. Let me take the driver's seat and let's go out of here, quickly. I won't trust you driving, you were knocked on your head too many times for one day, and besides you don't know where to go. And you," he turned to Eileen, "better go and sit behind."

"Do as he tells you," said Lennart. He changed seats with his friend and finally they drove away. Lennart wasn't really fully convinced of the trustworthiness of his friend and decided to keep an eye on him. Brian pretended not to notice anything; his attention was fully concentrated on the road in front of him. He was obviously in a hurry to leave the pirate camp as far behind as possible, driving with the maximum speed.

For some time nobody said a word, but then Lennart broke the silence.

"Where are we going?" he asked.

"To the eastern suburb of Sant Aargh," replied Brian. "I have some friends over there. They'll help us leave this accursed place. I'm getting heartily sick of it."

"Have you asked me what I want?" inquired Lennart. "Did I tell you I wanted to leave? Stop that car, immediately. I'm going back."

"You are crazy," said Brian. "Always has been. There is no road back to Istar or wherever your base is. You'll have to go through the jungle."

"So what?" asked Lennart.

"You'll be eaten by predators, that's what."

"You forget that I'm armed and can defend myself," insisted Lennart.

Brian for one moment took his eyes off the road and looked at his friend. "Do you know why the camp had to be evacuated?" he asked. "There is an epidemy in the area, one of our camps got devastated. An esquai epidemy." Lennart shrugged his shoulders.

"I was vaccinated against jungle fever."

"Vaccination doesn't help much against Black Esquai. You'll probably survive because of it, but since it's recurrent you'll keep having it, especially if you stay in a tropical climate. To get back to the base you'll have to cross the very area where the epidemy started. It's full of marshes and marshes are full of mosquitoes."

Lennart had heard about Black Esquai, of course, but at that moment he was not his rational self. "I don't care whether it's Black Esquai or not," he said stubbornly. "I have to get back to the base. You can take the girl and go to Sant Aargh or to the devil. I don't care."

"I want to go with you," said Eileen.

Lennart turned and looked at her. "Oh, but sweetheart, you can't. There is no place for a woman on a military base, and the road is dangerous, have you not heard?" She started crying softly.

"Very touching," said Brian sarcastically. "If women had any sense they wouldn't throw themselves at the likes of you. Anyway, if you insist, I'll drive you to the crossroads and then you'll have to take the way back to the North-West. In this manner you will have a shorter distance to walk than if you get out now. I took a map with me, you can have it. I'm not sure what are you going to eat though, and I wouldn't recommend you to drink from local springs but if you are bent on comitting suicide —."

"I have some supplies," said the girl. Lennart remembered that she had carried a big bag all the time, but he forgot to ask her what was in it.

"There is some water, too. We won't need it if we go to Sant Aargh."

"Thank you, dear," said Lennart.

When they parted the sun was rising in the sky. Eileen didn't even try to conceal her tears, but she didn't plead any more. Brian looked sober. "Won't you shake hands with me before you go?" he asked. Lennart did and then turned away with the map in his hand and followed the road leading in the right direction. He heard the car driving away but didn't turn even once though at that moment he felt profoundly alone.

It took him three days to get back to the base. When Lennart finally reached the borders of Varya he looked half starved and collapsed before they could bring him back to Istar. His concussion got worse because of the lack or rest and all his exertions and he developed a bad case of esquai as well.

Lennart spent more than a week in bed in a military hospital and the first couple of days wished for death, but eventually got better and started recovering. He was fervently hoping that he would be found unfit for active service, after all hadn't the doctor told him that he had to spend at least several months in a different climate?

This, however, was not the case. As long as the operation "Dawn Of Hope" lasted, the army needed its officers so when Lennart finally was in a state to leave the hospital ten days after he had been brought to it, he learned that he was sent to an orbital station where his task would be to enforce the blockade of the rebel city from the space, in cooperation with the representatives of the Royal Defence Force of Delta, and his only consolation was the fact that he was awarded another silver cross for going above and beyond the call of duty for his trip back to Istar through the jungle.

Chapter 9. Enforcing the Blockade

The station was built specially for the purposes of the blockade and since it was the creation of both Delta and Aargh it bore a rather pompous name “Solidarity.” It was used as a military base and stationed troops of both states, but the supreme command belonged to Delta, as it was essentially a Deltan project.

From “Solidarity” ships were sent to patrol the routes used by the pirates to bring the supplies to the rebel city and most of the crafts which tried to enter or leave Sant Aargh were detained and searched. There were a lot of clashes, especially in the beginning, but the combined forces of Aargh and Delta had a definite advantage and the noose around Sant-Aargh was tightening slowly but surely.

The life on the station was rather boring. There was not much to do. When off duty one couldn’t go to a tavern like in Istar, or enjoy the beauty of nature, unless he got a leave of several days and a chance to go to Aargh which was generally not possible unless you were wounded.

There was an officers’ club, a cinema, a bar, a library and a fitness center with a small swimming pool, and that was all. Most officers spent their time drinking and playing cards and Lennart didn’t form an exception. There for the first time in years he came into contact with his countrymen.

Westen, the language commonly used in Sector X was a derivative of Deltan and as a consequence of it most Aarghean officers spoke Deltan to some degree, but of course, it was Lennart’s mother tongue and anyone could hear it when he opened his mouth. That created a problem for him since he was not inclined to share his story with anyone.

Lennart had a good reason to conceal his name which was well-known on Delta, but people were bound to ask questions and so he had to think of something credible to tell them. He finally decided that if asked he’d say that his father was a Deltan businessman who had immigrated to Aargh where he married a local woman, and that was the story he told with a straight face when somebody asked him how it came that he spoke Deltan so well. To this Lennart usually added that his parents had died in an accident and that generally stopped people from asking further questions.

There were a couple of Deltans who doubted his words but they had the decency to conceal it, or may be there was something in Lennart’s eyes which prevented them from expressing those doubts. He was, however, not exactly popular by reason of his luck in playing poker which those who had lost their month's salary to him were inclined to attribute to something else than luck. Among them was Brendan Stewart, a captain of RDF.

One day he was sitting in the canteen and gloomily contemplating the amount of money he had lost the day before to captain Duncan. Someone approached his table and when Stewart raised his head he saw that it was his friend, Major Edward Hamilton. Hamilton was two and a half years older than Stewart and just turned thirty; he belonged to a higher social class, as his father was a lord, while Stewart's had been a parson, nevertheless, they were the best friends.

They came from the same part of Delta, attended the same private school and had played together as boys during school vacations, when Edward Hamilton spent the long summers in his father's country house. They fell in love at the same time, and both were engaged to be married when their deployment was over, the day that Brent Stewart was anticipating eagerly.

He was rather a romantic person and tended to view his fiancee as an angelic being. Edward was a more down-to-earth type; he had fallen in love before, but the objects of his affection didn't get his father's approval, until finally he was lucky enough to fall in love with a daughter of a prominent family. This time his father positively insisted he'd marry as soon as possible.

His marriage was thus both one of affection and of convenience, as it was normal for the men of his social standing. Brent, on the other hand, strongly believed in love as the only true basis for marriage. His father married his mother even though she was penniless, and they had been very happy together, until his father's untimely death two years ago.

The Reverend Stewart wasn't very wealthy, but the money he left was enough for his widow and daughter to live comfortably upon, and Margaret, Brent's sister, would have a good dowry when she married. Brent had a profession and could take care of himself. He had been saving money for his upcoming marriage and a card loss of the day before was rather a heavy blow to him, but when he complained to Edward, the latter just shrugged his shoulders.

"It was your own fault," he said indifferently. "And you were drunk as well. Never gamble when you're drunk, is one of my father's favorite maxims."

Brent could not agree with his friend. No, he hadn't been really that drunk, and he was generally considered a good player by everyone. That arrogant Aarghean half-caste simply didn't play fair. One person couldn't have so much luck, it was suspicious that he won all the time.

"Now you are being unfair, Brent, and you know it," retorted Edward. "I watched Duncan play and he lost several times as well. He simply has the good sense to quit when necessary, that's the secret of his success. But you, you go on stubbornly, the more you lose the more you seem determined to continue. That's how men become poor, you know. By the way, I don't think Duncan is a half-caste whatever stories about himself he chooses to tell. I think he is a pureblooded Deltan, what with those light blue eyes and blond hair. His face looks familiar, too, though I can't recollect where I've seen him before."

"That makes me think even worse of him," said Brent. "God knows why he left Delta and who his parents were."

"Whoever they may have been, they cared enough to give him a decent education," replied Edward, shrugging his shoulders. "He isn't the first youngest son who went to Aargh to try his luck and he won't be the last, either."

"Why would a man want to do such a thing?" asked Brent."And choose Aargh, of all places!"

"Why not?" laughed Edward. "The love of adventure is in our blood. I have thought about it myself, a couple of times. You can't comprehend it, Brent, because of your narrow bourgeois opinions." He always teased his friend about it, but it was a good-natured teasing. Edward Hamilton thought by himself that his friend's greatest problem was taking life too seriously.

This time, however, Brent wasn't inclined to joke at all. He wanted to say something, but before he could do it the door of the canteen opened and the man who had been the topic of their conversation walked in. He noticed both Stewart and Hamilton and nodded to them, then looked around searching for a free table. It was nearly lunch-time and the canteen was full.

Brent made a gesture inviting Captain Duncan to join them, and Lennart did. "Good afternoon, gentlemen," he said politely, sitting down at the table. "How do you do?"

"We have just been talking about you, Captain," said Brent, before his more polite friend could say a word.

"Really? I'm much honored to hear it," said Lennart. He spoke Deltan with a slight accent, but his speech was grammatically correct; and it betrayed a well-bred man. Edward looked closely at the captain's features and thought by himself that his first impressions had been correct. Before him was one of his countrymen, apparently from the North of Delta, one of his own class who had attended an expensive school.

When Edward reached this conclusion he decided it was a good idea to become more friendly with Duncan, "because we all have to stick together", was his vague thought. Unfortunately, his friend didn't share it and he was definitely searching for a reason to start a quarel.

"Yes," he continued, "we were just discussing your unusual luck in poker-playing, Captain."

"So you noticed it, too, didn't you?" asked Lennart rather insolently. " 'Unusual' is a wrong word to describe it, though. Some men are just more skillfull than others at playing poker. That's all." His intonation was unmistakably mocking.

It was evident to Edward that the captain had noticed his friend's attempts and wasn't in the mood to avoid a fight. He thought it was high time for him to interfere, but unfortunately, it was too late.

"Or may be they just don't play fair," retorted Brent angrily. Lennart looked at him and his blue eyes narrowed a bit. "Do you mean to imply, Captain, that I was cheating?" he asked, speaking slowly and distinctly.

"Gentlemen, stop it," said Edward. "Think of the consequences." Unfortunately, Brent wasn't able to stop any more. There was something in Lennart's manner of speaking that irritated him profoundly, and the fact that he had lost his temper, but the Aarghean adventure seeker hadn't, only infuriated him more.

"Yes, that's exactly what I meant," he said, "and I can repeat it."

"There is no need to," answered Lennart coldly. "I heard it well. There is only one answer to it, you know. I hope you had written your testament before you left for Aargh."

"You are both mad," interfered Edward. "You know that duels are forbidden, don't you? Why the hell are you behaving like this? Brent, think of your mother and Margaret and Elinor.... All this because of a small sum of money lost! And you, Captain, you should have not provoked him like this."

"It is a question who provoked whom," said Lennart dryly. "I distinctly remember last evening your friend here was hinting at the same thing."

"But he was drunk then," said Edward.

"Me too, but I behaved quite decently. And anyway, he isn't drunk any more."

Edward looked at both adversaries and understood that they were quite determined. "If you both insist," he said gloomily, "have it your way. I have warned you. It's better to have it over as soon as possible, so there is less chance for people to talk. I suggest we all go to the fitness center, if we are interrupted we can at least pretend that we were just practicing sword fighting."

They left the canteen together but nobody seemed to notice that things were out of the ordinary. Edward was the one who looked the most worried; his friend was still mad and didn't try hard to conceal it, while Lennart apparently didn't care at all. At this hour, the gym was empty. When they went in, Edward considered it his duty to undertake the last attempt to restore peace, but in vain.

The adversaries drew their swords and switched them on. After the first couple of clashes it became evident to Hamilton that the stranger was definitely much more skillful. He had a quicker reaction as well and stayed cool while Brent, who by some reason had expected an easy victory, was making one mistake after another. His anger seemed to have blinded him completely.

Edward bit on his lip and watched his friend retreat until he stood practically with his back to the wall. He made a last desperate attempt, but at that moment with a swift movement Lennart knocked the sword out of Stewart's hand and before the latter could do anything, the edge of the polariton blade was at his throat.

"I could ask you to apologize, but I think you have given me enough satisfaction for today," said Lennart taking away his sword. Brent was breathing heavily. For a moment, he thought the stranger was going to kill him.

"Where did you learn fencing, Captain?" asked Edward curiously.

"My father taught me. In his youth he was one of the best...he was quite good at it," finished Lennart.

"I'm sorry for the whole incident," continued Edward. "I don't know what possessed Brent today; he can be stubborn as a mule. I know he wouldn't apologize for the world, but I'll do it for both of us. It was a stupid business, and I'm happy it ended well. You are both unscathed. Will you shake hands with me, Captain?"

"You can call me Lennart if you wish to." Lennart smiled. "Of course, I will shake hands with you, Major."

"Edward," said Hamilton.

Brent listened to their talking and suddenly felt quite stupid. Of course, he hadn't been planning to kill the Aarghean, but he wanted to humiliate him. Brent was proud of his fencing skills, which were really good, but he had met someone who was clearly his superior. Yet, even though Duncan won he wouldn't go so far as to force him to admit it by demanding apologies and thus humiliating him even further. Brent thought that his own behavior and intentions came in a very unfavorable light compared to those of Duncan.

At that moment, Lennart turned and looked at him. "Captain Stewart, if you still think that I won unfairly I can give you your money back," he said and his eyes were laughing.

"You shouldn't tease him in this manner," interfered Edward. "Brent is a good guy, but he lacks a sense of humor." He said it in such a comical manner that both started laughing and Brent joined as well. Since that time the three became friends.

Chapter 10. The End of the War

"And so you never found out what had happened to your friend?" asked Brent as the three friends were sitting in the officers' club one evening.

"No," replied Lennart. "I do hope for him that he was able to leave Sant Aargh. By the way, keep in mind that you aren't supposed to tell the story to anyone else. I never mentioned meeting Alistair in my report. It could bring me in trouble as he was convicted of high treason."

"You know, we won't talk," said Edward.

"And the girl," continued Brent, "what do you think happened to her?"

Lennart shrugged his shoulders. "There is no way of knowing that, I'm afraid," he said. Truth be told, he kept thinking of the pretty slave now and then. Sometimes he saw her in his dreams. He wondered what bad luck made her a captive of the pirates. Lennart was convinced that she came from a good family.

"I have always thought that slavery should be abolished," Brent went on. He had the habit of preaching to others about the things they generally agreed upon but couldn't change. Edward always teased him about it, calling him a moral crusader and a defender of middle class values, which didn't seem to influence Brent in the slightest. He started a long tirade against the evils of slavery, not noticing that his friends were bored.

"I'm afraid there is nothing to be done about it," said Lennart. "Slavery is just a part of life on Aargh, whether one likes it or not."

"It's cruel and inhumane," insisted Brent.

"Aargh is a cruel place," replied Lennart. "That's a part of its charm, I guess."

"I have always wanted to visit it," remarked Edward. "I heard there is an annual slave market in summer and the girls are real beauties. May be I'll do it after the war is over." Here he looked at Brent, who was clearly shocked, and it cost him some effort to refrain from laughing. "And you, Len," he continued, "what are you planning to do when you are discharged?"

"I don't know yet," said Lennart. "My contract is nearly expired. I'm supposed to get benefits; a pension, medical insurance and financial assistance for starting a new career. I have been thinking of going into business."

"You should really come and visit us," said Brent. "Mother and Margaret will be delighted to meet you, and, of course, me and Elinor as well."

Lennart wanted to ask Brent if he wasn't afraid of his corrupting influence, but decided not to. His friend was a nice guy, but he did lack a sense of humor.

"I'll think of it," he promised instead.

That night he dreamed of Eileen. When he woke up and recollected it, he could only shake his head. It was stupid to care for a slave, especially one he would probably never see again. "I must be getting sentimental under Brent's influence," he thought.

The next day he and Edward were on duty together. The first half of their shift went on without anything out of the ordinary happening and then they had to search a ship which tried to leave Sant Aargh. It was a small trader looking innocent enough but one never knew what to expect. The ship had been intercepted and escorted to the station under the threat of annihilation.

Last time there were plenty of these small cargo ships trying to leave the doomed city, they were searched and if nothing objectionable was found, allowed to leave, but sometimes it was a pirate ship on a suicide mission and those who went to search it never came back; in other words, one couldn't be too careful.

Edward as higher in rank was in command, and Lennart followed him into the trader with a group of Aarghean soldiers. The crew consisted of a fat dark captain and his first mate, both natives of Volcan, who stated that they had come to Sant Aargh on business in the first days of the war, had been detained in the city due to circumstances and now finally decided it was time to try and leave it, they didn't have any cargo but took two passengers, an old couple who gave away their life savings in order to escape.

The couple appeared to be in their sixties, a man dressed in rags, with a dark beard, and a woman whose face was covered with a black cloth, so that one could only see her deep blue eyes. Lennart let Hamilton lead the interrogation, his soldiers looked around uneasily, some of them quite nervous. Just last week a ship like this one became a common grave for both those who entered to search it and the crew.

"We be peaceful people," repeated the ship owner in broken Westen. "We nothing to do with pirates. We no smugglers." His voice sounded whiny.

"Tell your men to search the ship, Captain," said Hamilton.

Lennart gave his orders, four men left to do the searching, four others stayed with them. There was a pause when they were all waiting for the search team to come back, finally they returned and reported that they hadn't found any smuggleware or indeed any cargo at all.

"Me speak the truth," whined the captain of the ship. Lennart and Edward looked at each other. Edward then turned to the passengers. "How old are you and what is your profession?" he asked in Westen, but the man only shook his head. There was something familiar in the way he did it.

"He speak no Westen," the ship owner informed them.

"Then you interrogate him, Captain," ordered Edward.

Lennart looked at the old man's face. It was wrinkled and dirty, and he had in general a dishevelled look. "Your age and your profession?" asked Lennart.

"Sixty three," he answered in a low voice, speaking Aarghean with a strange nasal accent. He told Lennart he was a merchant in fabrics, who had sold his business at a tremendous loss to himself only to be able to leave the planet. Yes, that woman was his wife. They were going to live with his family on Volcan.

"Tell her to show her face," ordered Hamilton.

"That no possible," interfered the fat ship owner. "The Volcan lady no show her face to strange men, big shame."

"I need to see her face," insisted Hamilton. "I must know if it is a lady."

The fat captain frowned and his mate made a threatening gesture. The old man stood in front of his wife, and the woman (Lennart was sure it was a woman) looked at him pleading and there was something in her eyes which made Lennart dizzy for a moment. He had seen those eyes before. He looked at Edward and spoke Deltan, so that they would not be understood.

"I think, it's better to let them go, Ted. Those Volcanis have the strangest opinions about honor, and can be dangerous when cornered. Why risking bloodshed?"

"This so-called lady could be one of the pirate chiefs trying to escape," insisted Hamilton.

"I don't think so," said Lennart. "And even should it be so...remember what happened to Team A last week?"

"We should have searched them before searching their ship," said Hamilton. "But you are probably right. They look innocent enough."

He switched to Westen and informed the detainees that they were free to follow their course. The soldiers hardly concealed their relief when they got the orders to retreat. As they were leaving the ship Lennart looked back and caught the eye of the old man. "Good bye, Brian," he thought. "Now I have paid my debt to you."

A couple of weeks later Lennart turned twenty six. Brendan and Edward went to congratulate him and found their friend in a fit of rage. Lennart was staring at the sheet of paper in his hand and swearing in Aarghean, as it was his habit.

"What's this all about?" inquired Edward. Lennart calmed down a bit and explained that when he had come to his room he found an official letter which informed him that though his contract had expired he couldn't retire as long as the war was going on.

"A nice birthday present," he said bitterly.

"Never mind," tried Brent to comfort him. "The war can't go on indefinitely. The end of the pirates is near."

"I simply hate all about the service," said Lennart gloomily. "I'm sick of it. All my life I have been doing nothing else but following orders." He now understood how Brian had felt. That night he went to the bar and got terribly drunk.

The war ended for Lennart sooner than he had expected. The next week, Edward had to interrupt his lunch to oversee the emergency transport taking the wounded back to Aargh. A routine ship search turned into a bloody battle, several soldiers were dead and some had been wounded. With a shock Edward recognized a man lying on a stretcher as his friend.

Lennart's face was deathly gray, but he tried to smile when he saw Edward. He had been injured in an explosion and there was a real chance that he'd lose his left arm. He had lost a lot of blood as well and his life was in danger.

"God, Len, try to hold on," said Edward.

"I will," promised Lennart. His voice sounded coarse and as he was speaking a grimace of pain distorted his face. As he was taken away Edward prayed that his friend would lose his consciousness, which in fact happened.

"I don't think I'll ever see him again," he said to himself, but here he was mistaken.

Part II
DELTA

Chapter 1. Lennart Takes a Decision

Lennart didn't die and didn't lose his arm, but he spent more than a month in the hospital and when he finally got better the war was over. He had always had an exceptionally good health and always recovered quickly, but there is a limit to what a man can take and Lennart seemed to have reached it. Though he kept his arm, he was aware that he never would be able to recover completely from his wound; in fact, despite several operations and the advanced methods of treatment Lennart knew he could anticipate the day when he wouldn't be able to use it at all.

"You shouldn't get too upset about it now," the surgeon told him. "We are talking about a long period of time, may be thirty years or thereabout, but the prognose is usually negative."

"There is some comfort in thinking I probably won't live so long," muttered Lennart as a response.

"I don't see why not," said the surgeon, "unless you go on some wild-goose chase looking for adventures again."

Lennart wasn't planning on doing anything wild. In fact, his arm didn't bother him that much, he could still use it and it generally only gave him trouble when the weather changed, much worse were the incapacitating headaches he got due to what the doctors called by the long name of "the medically unexplained multisymptom illness", which seemed to affect a lot of veterans coming home from war, so that the common name for it was "the veteran syndrome."

"You come from Delta, don't you?" asked an old doctor who had been treating him. "Your native climate will do you a lot of good. Why don't you go and spend a couple of months with your family?"

"I have no family," said Lennart.

"But you must have some friends there," insisted the doctor. "You just need to find peace of mind again; besides, the tropical climate isn't good for you. Your contract has been prolonged for half a year, which means that you still have four months of full pay before you officially retire. Why not use your time wisely?"

"I will think of it," promised Lennart.

It was a strange thing but now that he finally was free he didn't know what to do. In order to use his benefits fully he had to choose an occupation which would entitle him to the bonus money from the government, but Lennart had no idea what he'd rather do. It had to be a desk job in any case, since he wouldn't be able to perform physical labor in his present state, but the problem was that he didn't have any profession outside that of a soldier.

The only job he had before was his brief employment in construction.Years ago, before he came to Aargh, Lennart had done a semester at a university, studying economics. He had been quite good at his studies, and that fact gave him a vague idea about the employment in the financial sphere, but the thought of being an accountant in some company wasn't particularly thrilling.

Anyway, he still had more than four months of the sick leave and could just enjoy life and delay taking a decision. Lennart thought about the doctor's advice. He remembered that Brent had repeatedly invited him to come and spend some time with his family after the war was over.

Lennart didn't hear anything from either him or Edward after his return back to Aargh, but he presumed that both stayed alive and returned home safely. In fact, now they both were probably preparing for their weddings, or may be married already. Lennart wondered what kind of woman Elinor was that she inspired such poetic feelings in his friend.

The more he thought about the idea to spend some time on Delta the more he liked it. And really, why shouldn't he do it, he thought. After all, more than eight years have passed.... And Brent lives in another part of the planet.... Brendan repeated his address many times so that Lennart knew it by heart. He lived in the central part of the main continent of Delta, not so far away from the capital which bore a poetic name The Star of the North.

The village where Brent came from was called Stockdale and though Lennart had never visited it, he had been to the area once, long ago. His decision was taken. Citizens of Aargh didn't need any visas to travel to Delta and the only thing he had to do was to buy a ticket.

Ten days later Lennart was standing outside the beautiful modern building of the chief space haven of the Northern Star, breathing fresh air and looking around. It was nice for once to see a sky of a deep blue color instead of one with the purple tint in it. It was just the beginning of spring and the wind seemed chilly to Lennart, accustomed to the warm climate, but the weather was good, dry and sunny, while on Aargh the rain season just started.

Lennart felt much better already. He took a taxi to the train station, then the train to Stockdale. It was about one and a half hour trip and Lennart spent it reading a newspaper he had bought while waiting for the train. On the front page there was a story about the parliamentary debates and about the speech one of the leaders of the opposition party had delivered the day before.

It was around five o'clock when the train finally arrived to the village of his destination. Lennart stepped outside and looked around. There were several people getting out together with him, mostly women who had gone to the capital for shopping.

It was strange for Lennart to see women wearing colorful dresses and frilly hats and talking to men. On Aargh, decent women were never seen in company of men other than their immediate family. In fact, one hardly saw them at all, and when they ventured outside, they would cover their clothes with black cloaks and their hair with black scarves. Some even went so far as to wear veils; and they normally would never talk to strange men.

Lennart finally chose a motherly looking middle-aged lady and asked her the way to Milford Street. She looked at him surprised. His accent betrayed a foreigner, just as much as his tropical suntan. "It's not that far away from the station," she said. "I'm going that way myself, you could join me."

Lennart did, though he quickly regretted it. The lady by the name of Mrs Mills asked him all sorts of questions and by the end of their ten minutes walk got practically the whole story of their friendship out of Lennart. He breathed a sigh of relief when she finally pointed to a two-storied cottage standing at the end of the street with the words: "Here you are, Captain. It's good that you came, poor Captain Stewart sure could use some friendly consolation."

Lennart wondered what that meant, but considered it wise not to ask any questions. In fact, he was glad finally to be able to escape the interrogation, so he just walked in the direction of the cottage, opened the fence door, and before ringing the door bell, thought that it was exactly as he had imagined it would be. Exactly as Lennart saw it in his dreams so often.

He suddenly felt a strange emotion, and shook his head trying to suppress it. There were some things it was better not to dwell upon too long. He rang the door bell and heard the approaching footsteps. An old pleasantly looking lady who, as Lennart correctly determined, was a housekeeper, opened the door.

She looked at the stranger, surprised. Lennart coughed, he suddenly had difficulty speaking, but he pulled himself together. "Good evening," he said, and his accent became stronger, as it was usual for him when he was nervous. "Is Captain Stewart home?"

Chapter 2. Meeting The Stewarts

The housekeeper looked surprised but nodded her head and inquired: "How should I announce you, sir?"

"It's better if you don't," said Lennart, who partially regained his confidence, "I want to surprise him. You see, I am an old friend of his."

The housekeeper nodded, even though she didn't look entirely convinced of the propriety of such a manner of action and invited him to come in. Lennart followed her through the narrow corridor into the living-room. It wasn't really big, but it looked very cosy, with a fire place and a piano, and there was the family all together drinking tea: a middle-aged lady who was apparently Brendan's mother, a young girl of about eighteen, and Brendan himself.

They were talking but the conversation stopped when Lennart entered the room, and they all looked at their visitor. Lennart nearly laughed at Brendan's face expression, he actually dropped his teacup and stood up staring at Lennart as if the latter were a ghost. He then tried to say something but the words evidently failed him.

His mother and sister looked at both men not being able to understand the scene. The surprise was more successful than Lennart could have expected, and instead of all the polite words he had been thinking of he ran to his friend who looked as if he were going to faint and asked, "Brent, what's wrong with you?" He wanted to say, "what the hell", but remembered the presence of the ladies just in time.

Lennart's voice seemed to break the charm and Brendan finally got his tongue back. "So you are alive?" he asked, still speaking with difficulty.

"Of course, I am," said Lennart. "Did you have any reason to believe otherwise?"

"I thought...I was sure you were dead," said Brent. "Ted told me. He said you wouldn't make it and then we both heard nothing from you."

"That explains a lot of things," laughed Lennart, "but I'm alive and I decided to accept your invitation. I hope you don't regret inviting me, do you?"

"No, of course, not," replied Brent.

Now that he was finally convinced his friend was not a ghost, he was obviously glad to see him and turned to his mother and sister. "Mother, Margaret," he said, "this is Captain Lennart Duncan, the friend I had told you so much about. He is alive," added Brent, as if there were still some doubts about the fact.

Mrs Stewart rose to her feet and cordially shook hands with Lennart. "I'm glad to meet you, Captain," she said. "We heard so much about you. Welcome to Delta." She was a pleasant-looking woman of about fifty, with auburn hair starting to turn gray and brown eyes, and Brendan looked very much like her. Margaret, his sister, was blond and had gray eyes and lively features. She came to shake hands, too.

After that Lennart was seated into a chair, they poured tea for him, gave him the biggest piece of cake and in general, surrounded him with so much care as he hadn't got since he had been a little boy. One couldn't say he did not like it.

Lennart wasn't shy by nature, but he had spent too long a time on Aargh and wasn't accustomed to the company of what he called "decent women", especially if they were as young and pretty as Margaret. On Aargh, one didn't flirt with young women from good families, one married them; as for girls from not-so-good familes, one usually didn't spend much time flirting with them either, or courting them, or talking about anything serious, for that matter. As a result of that, Lennart's manners around females got rather rusty. It was easier for him to communicate with Mrs Stewart who was old enough to be his mother, but he could not bring himself to address Margaret directly, or even look at her at all.

The girl, on the other hand, showed him a lot of attention and kept giggling which only increased Lennart's embarassment. Mrs Stewart, who had noticed his uneasiness, tried to make him more comfortable, poured him more tea, and asked him about his trip, and Brent wanted to know how it came that Lennart was still alive.

When he finally satisfied their curiosity and drank by his own estimation not less than two liters of tea, he was allowed to retire to a room shown to him by the housekeeper whose name was Mrs Jones, to take a bath and change for dinner.

When Lennart was planning his trip he had some doubts about the propriety of inflicting himself upon strangers for the whole length of four months and decided to stay in a hotel, but when he only mentioned it, Mrs Stewart wouldn't even want to hear about the plan. He had to stay with them during the whole length of his visit, and that was that.

Thus Lennart was given the best (and only) guest room with the adjoining bathroom. The bathroom he would have to share with Brent though, but he hardly thought it an inconvenience. While he was changing his travel clothes for a fresh shirt and slacks, the Stewart family were talking below.

"Your friend is a very nice young man, with pleasant manners," said Mrs Stewart. "By your description, I imagined him somewhat different though."

"He is very cute," said Margaret, "but he avoided me the whole time. Why is it, Mother?"

"It's probably because he is an Aarghean, my dear," replied Mrs Stewart. "On Aargh, I read, ladies don't spend time with gentlemen other than their husbands or near male relatives. It must be difficult for him to get accustomed to our traditions. You must give him some time."

During dinner Lennart mainly talked to his friend, and Margaret kept silence, which gave him a chance to get accustomed to her company, so that he soon started feeling more at ease and his accent nearly disappeared. He asked Brendan about Edward Hamilton and learned that Ted was presently staying with his family in the capital, preparing for his wedding which was to take place in about three months.

"Well, that's fine news," said Lennart. "And what about you, Brent? When is your turn?"

At these words, Brendan suddenly turned rather pale and looked away, and Mrs Stewart looked embarrassed while Lennart could swear that Margaret got tears in her eyes. Lennart suddenly remembered the words of Mrs Mills: "poor captain Stewart needs some friendly consolation," or something to the point and a terrible suspicion arose in his mind.

"Elinor," he asked, "she is not...I hope nothing happened to her? She is not sick?"

Here Margaret made a strange sound and left the table and Mrs Stewart went after her.

"Elinor is all right," finally replied Brendan in a muffled voice. "She is going to get married soon. But not to me."

"Oh," said Lennart, shocked. "Did you quarel?"

Brendan, still avoiding looking at his friend started telling him the story of his disappointment in love. It appeared that Elinor got tired of waiting and during Brendan's absence found a man who was wealthier. She didn't inform him about breaking the engagement and Brendan only learned about it upon coming back a month ago. His sister felt for him strongly and still could not get over the fact, and from what Lennart figured out, his friend couldn't get over it, either.

"I'm sorry," said Lennart, "had I known how the things stood between you, I wouldn't have mentioned her name."

"It doesn't matter," Brent smiled faintly. "You were bound to know, sooner or later. I'd just want to ask you never to talk about it when my sister is present. She is so sensitive."

"Of course, I won't," assured him Lennart.

At that point, Mrs Stewart and Margaret returned and the rest of the dinner went by without any events.

Lennart's visit to Stewarts was soon known in the whole village and as a result they had company every evening for the coming several weeks, but despite nosy neighbors Lennart enjoyed his stay at his friend's more than he had ever expected. The weather was getting warmer and the three young people would take long walks together, he would play tennis with his friend or his pretty sister, and in the evenings they would play the piano and sing.

Lennart's health improved tremendously, his headaches subsided and the left arm didn't give him any trouble at all. The color got back to his cheek and he put on weight and wasn't looking so thin and worn out as when he had first entered the Stewarts' house. Of all the neighbors the one who spent the most time with them was Miss Nerts, a particular friend of Mrs Stewart, an old spinster lady of about sixty five years of age.

She often spent evenings with them, and that particular evening was not an exception. Lennart and Margaret were sitting behind the piano together. Lennart had been taught to play the instrument but it was years since he had touched the keys and Margaret insisted on giving him lessons. Lennart was not blind and realized that the girl liked him, which put him in a rather difficult position.

He liked her, too, she was young and fresh as a rose; and frankly, he being just a mortal man, enjoyed her attention, but she was his friend's sister and a lady. The affection was present on her side but he wasn't sure it was really present on his and if it were, what then? Could he marry her, in his circumstances? Would her mother agree to her only daughter's marriage to a stranger without any credentials? What could he offer her?

Those were the uncomfortable questions Lennart had to ask himself, but that late April evening he wasn't in the mood to try and answer them. He simply enjoyed the spring and her company, and felt himself much younger, as if he were eighteen again and still thought the world was his for taking.

Margaret was laughing. "I have just played you my favorite song," she said. "Now it's your turn, Captain. You have been making a lot of progress lately."

"OK," said Lennart, he thought a bit and started playing, first uncertainly touching the keys, but then more sure of himself. He stopped noticing what happened around him, for a moment he allowed his thoughts to go back to the past, to the time when he had been happy once.

Margaret wasn't the only one who had noticed a strange expression on his face. Miss Nerts looked at Lennart with more than her usual curiosity, too. When he finished playing it seemed to him that he had just awoken out of a dream.

Lennart looked around and Mrs Stewart clapped her hands. "It was beautiful, Captain," she said. "Where did you learn that melody? I remember it was popular about ten years ago."

"It was my mother's favorite song," said Lennart. "She taught me to play it. Will you excuse me, please?" He stood up and went into the garden.

"Are you sure you know all there is to know about your visitor, my dear?" asked Miss Nerts quietly.

"Oh yes," replied Mrs Stewart absent-mindedly. "His parents died in a car crash, poor thing, when he was still very young. It must have been a terrible shock to him."

Miss Nerts nodded but didn't look convinced.

Chapter 3. A Business Proposal

The first week of May came and Brendan became visibly depressed. Elinor was going to be married soon. Lennart kept an eye on his friend and noticed that he was getting gloomier by the day. One day he disappeared without saying a word to anyone and came home late in the evening, drunk, much to the dismay of Mrs Stewart.

Lennart wasn't the type to force a confidence out of anyone but his friend couldn't keep a secret for a long time and so Lennart found out that Brent had gone to see Elinor and try and persuade her to marry him instead of her current fiance. When she refused, he went to a bar and got drunk.

Lennart could only shake his head. He couldn't imagine why Brendan would even want her back, after Elinor had showed what kind of woman she was, let alone humiliate himself by begging her to take him back. Lennart was too proud to even contemplate this course of action, but he knew his friend's character and refrained from any remarks.

The week before Elinor's wedding Brent was drunk practically every evening. Mrs Stewart looked worried and taking Lennart aside asked him if he could try and speak to her son.

"After he came back and found out about Elinor's unfaithfulness, he seemed to have lost all sense of purpose," she complained. "At least if he were still in the military, he'd have something to do, but now he just sits home and thinks about his misfortunes."

Lennart promised her to use his good influence on Brent, but this conversation made him think of something else. Though he considered Brent's behaviour ridiculous, he could understand his friend to some extent. Lennart experienced the same feeling of the lack of purpose.

His leave was drawing to the end and the issue of his future employment occupied his mind. Lennart by nature was an active type and though he thoroughly enjoyed his visit to the Stewarts he was starting to feel restless. A nature like his needed something to do. Now a plan started forming in his mind. Lennart decided to try his hand at business.

There were three things that made Aargh rich, they said: weapon trade, diamond trade and slave trade, and Lennart decided that the weapon trade was the way to go. His plan was to have a small company which would buy weapons on Aargh and then deliver them to other planets and sell them there.

Lennart had friends on Aargh who could help him start and he had saved quite a bit of money, but it was still not enough to pay all the expenses and to buy a decent cargo ship as well. He also needed a good pilot, because his own pilot skills were not that great and also because in his state of health he realized he could not undertake long trips alone.

Brendan had inherited some money from his father, and he was an excellent pilot, too; he was also desperately in need of distraction. Lennart, who had an optimistic nature, thought that work would heal his friend's wounds and so he offered Brendan to become his partner. They would go to Aargh together and come back rich as princes.

Brendan didn't seem thrilled at first, but then he read the news about Elinor's wedding having taken place and decided he wanted to get as far as possible from Delta and so he agreed to Lennart's plan. Mrs Stewart was a little worried about her son going to Aargh; she wouldn't want to hurt Captain Duncan's feelings for the world, but wasn't Aargh a den of sin and iniquity?

Margaret, of course, felt nothing for Lennart's leaving them, either. Lennart patiently explained to both ladies that they would run a perfectly legal business, come in contact with decent folks and live in a nice part of the city; and he had to leave anyway, whether alone or with Brent.

Mrs Stewart thought it over and decided that it was probably for the best and gave her blessing. Lennart would go to Aargh alone at first and complete all the necessary formalities, and Brent would join him later; but before that they both were invited to attend Edward Hamilton's wedding.

The ceremony was simple but elegant, the bride looked charming in her white dress, the church bells were ringing and everybody was happy, except Brendan who looked as if he were attending a funeral instead of a wedding. Lennart, who was sensitive to the rules of decorum, tried to point out the impropriety of such behavior to his friend, but soon realized he was just wasting his time and left Brendan alone.

During the reception he got a chance to talk to Edward. Having congratulated him heartily, Lennart talked about his plans for the future.

"I personally think it's a great idea," said Edward. "And it will do poor Brent a lot of good, too. He desperately needs something to occupy himself with. Sad story, that with Elinor. By the way, where is he?"

"I have no idea," answered Lennart. "I hope he isn't getting drunk."

"At this time of the day?" inquired Hamilton, scandalized. "During a wedding reception? That would be too bad."

"I'd better go and search for him," suggested Lennart, who by some strange reason felt responsible for his friend's good behavior, "before he gets a chance to do something really stupid, like insulting one of those MP's you invited. It could cause a parliamentary crisis."

Ted laughed and they parted, Lennart went through the hall searching for his friend, but couldn't find him anywhere. He didn't notice that he was being observed by a dark-haired man with a knife scar on his cheek. Brent was nowhere to be seen, and Lennart returned back, exasperated and with the intention to inform Edward that he washed his hands in advance of anything Brent would do that day; but he didn't get a chance to express his feelings on the issue as Edward came to meet him, but not alone: the dark-haired man with a scar accompanied him.

Edward was obviously in a hurry, and instead of a formal introduction he just said briefly: "Len, this is Mr Thompson, my father's friend. Mr Thompson is an investment banker and he is interested in your project."

Lennart was surprised but before he could ask any questions, Edward already disappeared. Mr Thompson was a man about twenty years Lennart's senior, and the latter thought that he didn't look like an investment banker at all. For some time they studied each other and Mr Thompson was the first to break the silence.

"Captain Duncan, there are some business matters I want to discuss with you," he said, in a voice of a man accustomed to give orders and be obeyed. "Don't you think it's better if we go into the garden? There nobody will disturb us."

"Very well," answered Lennart who became even more surprised.

The man seemed vaguely familiar, but he couldn't remember where he had seen him before. They went into the garden and sat on a bench near the fountain. Mr Thompson looked at Lennart again and smiled: "Good afternoon, Lord Alex," he said. "I'm glad to see you alive and in good health."

Lennart changed his color and swallowed hard, unable to speak for a moment, but then regained his self-control and smiled. "You must be mistaken, sir," he said, but Thompson shook his head.

"I'm not and we both know it."

The way in which he said it convinced Lennart there was no use pretending. "You seem to know who I am, but I don't know who you are," he replied.

"Here you are wrong, because we have met before, in your father's house," said Thompson. "Only then I was introduced under the name Ferrash."

Lennart looked at him more attentively and nodded. "I thought I had seen you before, but I wasn't sure. So Thompson isn't your real name, is it? I guess that investment banker isn't your real occupation, either? What exactly do you want from me?"

Thompson-Ferrash smiled. "You aren't very polite," he said, "but I'll satisfy your curiosity. Here is my card." He took it out of his pocket and gave to Lennart. Lennart read the contents and looked inquiringly. "A colonel of the military intelligence of Delta," he said slowly. "That figures, but what business matters do you want to discuss with me?"

"I heard your story from Hamilton, and got interested," said Ferrash. "That company of yours, I mean. I'm going to make you an offer,

my lord."

"Don't call me 'my lord'," protested Lennart, "it sounds ridiculous, call me Captain Duncan."

"As you wish," agreed Ferrash, "though I'd say one shouldn't try to escape his problems but rather confront them...Anyway, it's not relevant to me how you desire to be called as long as you agree with my proposal. I offer you a job."

"A job," repeated Lennart, stunned. "...are you serious?"

"Perfectly," assured him Ferrash. "I offer you a position as an officer in the military intelligence. What would you say to this?"

"I would say that I refuse," said Lennart. "I have no desire to join the army again. By the way, why do you want to have me?"

"Because we need your company, that's why," replied Ferrash. "And we need a man we could trust implicitely, young, energetic, intelligent, with a sense of duty to his fatherland."

"I'm sure there are plenty of young men to choose from," said Lennart.

"It's essential that he knows Aarghean and has friends on that planet who could help, and being a citizen of Aargh is a bonus as well, plus a military experience," added Ferrash. "To sum it up, you are an ideal candidate, Captain."

"Well, I hate to disappoint you," said Lennart who was getting irritated, "but the answer is still 'no'."

"It's amazing to me that a man of your origin and position in society would leave it all and become a soldier of fortune on Aargh, but then refuse to serve his own fatherland in her hour of need," said Ferrash solemnly.

"I didn't know it was the hour of need for my fatherland," persisted Lennart. "Is the war going to start? And since you know who I am it shouldn't be difficult to understand why I left. It was my personal business anyway."

"You chose to serve a foreign country, but wouldn't serve your own," said Ferrash. "Some would say it amounts to treason."

"If you say this again you'll have to fight with me," declared Lennart angrily.

"You will probably lose," replied Ferrash coldly. "I'm still quite good with the sword. As for the hour of need, have you heard of the situation on Tarna?"

"I'm not interested in politics. Besides, what has Tarna to do with it all?" inquired Lennart.

"Tarna is suffering under the merciless rule of Uranius, a planet which gets more powerful and dangerous by the day," said Ferrash. "What would you say to that, Captain?"

"I have always had sympathy for the rebels on Tarna," answered Lennart. "But I still don't understand what it has to do with me? I'm not a Tarnian, thank Heaven."

"It has to do with curbing the growing power and ambition of Uranius," stated Ferrash and at that moment Lennart thought he started understanding.

"You mean that you are planning to support the separatists on Tarna in order to weaken Uranius?" he asked. Ferrash smiled, satisfied.

"Brilliant, Captain," he said.

"And my company—."

"Is needed as a legal instrument of supplying them with weapons. Weapons which will be produced on Aargh, not on Delta, so that there will be no direct connection."

"I see," said Lennart.

"Now that you know everything and hopefully understand the importance of the operation for your country, is your answer still 'no', Captain?"

Lennart said nothing. His common sense told him he should refuse, but the appeal to his sense of duty wasn't in vain. "You are an idiot," said a voice in his head. "Think of the implications of your decision." Lennart hesitated, then looked at Ferrash. "I accept your offer, Colonel," he said quietly and felt as if he had just signed his own death sentence.

Chapter 4. Miss Nerts

Ferrash smiled, visibly satisfied. "I knew I could count on your sense of patriotism, Lord Alex."

"What do you expect me to do?" asked Lennart, rather gloomily.

"You will leave for Aargh this week," instructed Ferrash. "There you will come in contact with a man by the name of Smith, who will give you further instructions. Since you now serve the King of Delta, you must have a Deltan passport. I guess you haven't kept yours?"

"I lost it," lied Lennart. In reality, he had burned it the day he got Aarghean citizenship.

"On which name do you want to have your new passport?"

"On the name of Lennart Duncan, twenty six, born on Aargh," said Lennart. "I thought it was obvious."

Ferrash sighed. "If you allow me to give you a piece of advice, Captain—."

Lennart's face became hard and his light blue eyes got a steely expression: "I want you to understand one thing, Colonel. My personal affairs are my own business and I'm not going to discuss them with anyone, not even with you. Is that clear?"

"Perfectly clear," assured him Ferrash. "You will get the passport on the name you wish."

"And my father or anyone of my family must know nothing about the real identity of Captain Duncan. They think me dead and let it stay so."

"I won't tell anyone," promised Ferrash. "I gather you haven't seen your father?"

"On the television last week," said Lennart. "He is one of the opposition leaders, isn't he? He was making a speech which criticised the new budget."

"I thought you were not interested in politics," reminded him Ferrash.

"I couldn't avoid it since the Stewarts wanted to watch the debates."

Here is one problem," said Ferrash. "You are intending to make Brendan Stewart your partner, aren't you?"

"What's wrong with it?" inquired Lennart.

"He must know nothing about the whole business," said Ferrash resolutely.

"But he could be a great asset —." started Lennart, but the colonel interrupted him.

"Stewart drinks. And when he drinks, he talks. The whole town knows the story of his misfortunes with Elinor, or what-was-her-name. I'd prefer you to get rid of him entirely."

"It's impossible," said Lennart coldly. "Brent Stewart is my friend and we made a business agreement. I can't break my word. Besides, I need his money and I need a good pilot. I can't fly alone."

"In any case, it's your responsibility to ensure that Stewart knows nothing about the real nature of your work," declared Ferrash, and the manner in which he said it prevented Lennart from making any further objections.

At that moment a lonely figure entered the garden, looked around uncertainly, went in the direction of the fountain, stumbled and fell into it.

"Here is your business partner, Captain," said Ferrash. "If I were you, I'd take him out of the fountain and bring home as soon as possible."

He stood up and Lennart did the same. The person in the fountain was making desperate attempts to get out of the undeep water, but rather unsuccessfully.

"There is an address on the card I gave you," went Ferrash on. "I expect you tomorrow at ten in my office where we will continue our conversation. Good-bye."

The next morning Brendan stayed in bed with a headache and it was not difficult for Lennart to invent a story as to why he needed to go to the capital alone. He said that he had to buy some things for his upcoming journey home and it was enough. Mrs Stewart kept musing about her son's propensity to get drunk and Margaret was occupied with the thought of Lennart leaving them. Neither asked for details and after a hasty breakfast Lennart left for the Northern Star.

He had no trouble in finding a gray high building where he had an appointment with Ferrash and he was allowed inside after showing the card and giving his name. At ten exactly he entered Ferrash's office.

"I won't keep you long, Captain," assured him the latter, "but yesterday we had no time to discuss certain formalities. Your contract with the Republic of Aargh has officially expired, hasn't it?"

"It expired the day before yesterday," answered Lennart.

"That's fine," said Ferrash and pushed a sheet of paper towards him. "Here is your new contract. Read it and sign below. You will start with the same rank you got in the Aarghean army, and, of course, you can get promoted. You will get all official benefits, a pension in case of disability; in case of your death your widow will get a pension as well.

"I'm not married," said Lennart scanning through the document.

"I know," smiled Ferrash. "But it can change."

Lennart took a pen but before signing paused. "I think I have to inform you, Colonel, that I was found unfit for active service."

"You'll have to undergo a medical examination, of course," replied Ferrash, "but I don't think it will be a problem. For our purposes, you are healthy enough."

Lennart signed the paper and then he had to get upon one knee in front of the Deltan flag and to swear the oath of allegiance to the kingdom.

"Raise your right hand and repeat after me," instructed him Ferrash.

"...in the name of the Kingdom I swear by my honor to fight and to die, if necessary, cheerfully; knowing that no destiny is better than to give one's life for his Fatherland; so help me God."

After that Lennart had to undergo a medical examination. He was put through the scanner and got his blood examined, and the doctor looked at his left arm's scans and shook his head. "It will get worse with time, I'm afraid," he said.

"I know," answered Lennart.

"You have a very high concentration of antibodies to Esquai in your blood," continued the doctor. "When in a tropical climate during the rain season, you need anti-fever medication."

"I was told so far," assured him Lennart.

"Those headaches of yours, do you have them often?"

"Since I've come to Delta, only once."

"You need to avoid stress," informed him the doctor.

He typed something. Lennart looked above his shoulder at the computer screen and read, "Fit for active service". "They really need me desperately," he thought but wisely refrained from making any remarks.

That evening would be his last on Delta. The next day he was leaving. They were to spend it in the narrow family circle, with only Miss Nerts as a visitor, but she was practically a part of the family. Margaret looked very beautiful in her long white dress, with a ribbon in her hair, but she was sad and as a result, silent.

Brendan was still suffering from the consequences of the hangover. Lennart had things on his mind to think about, and wasn't very talkative, either. At half past ten Miss Nerts finally rose up. "It has been a very pleasant evening," she said, "but I think it's better to make it not too late, considering that Captain Duncan has to leave early in the morning. By the way, Captain," she addressed Lennart, "would you mind seeing me off to my house? It's so dark and I'd rather not go alone."

"Of course, madam," said Lennart politely. Miss Nerts usually got escorted back by Brendan as the host, but today he was obviously not in his best condition.

They walked through the narrow lane leading to Miss Nerts's house and at the door Lennart was going to say good-bye, but to his surprise, Miss Nerts invited him to come in. "There is something I want to show you, Captain," she said. Curious, Lennart went inside.

Chapter 5. The Shadow of the Past

It was Thursday evening and the servants had their night off, so that they were alone. Lennart entered the living-room and looked around. It was cosy, though rather old-fashioned, with dark furniture and fluffy carpets, and family photos on the walls. In the center of the room there was a low coffee table with a newspaper lying on it.

"Will you sit down, Captain?" asked Miss Nerts. Lennart installed himself in a comfortable, oversized armchair and his eyes fell upon the paper on the table. It was a photocopy of a newspaper from nine years ago. On the front page there was a picture of himself and the title read: "Son's Testimony Saves Father from the Gallows. Lord N. found not guilty by the jury."

Lennart looked up and his eyes met Miss Nerts's. "So you know," he said slowly.

"Yes, Lord Alex," nodded the old woman. "I recognized you. After all, you haven't changed that much, only become older."

"I shouldn't have come over here," said Lennart bitterly. "It was a mistake. I thought after all those years people would forget, but they never do. Of course, my picture appeared in all the newspapers."

"Past often haunts us," said Miss Nerts thoughtfully.

"I know what you must think of me," continued Lennart, not paying much attention to her words, his eyes fixed on the picture in the paper. "After all, I committed perjury, but what else could I do? I wouldn't have lied only to save his life, but I had to think about family honor. Harry just got his second son and Peter's wife was expecting. I thought about their future, how would their children grow up with the knowledge that their grandfather was hanged for murdering their grandmother?"

"It must have been a very difficult decision for you to take," said Miss Nerts sympathetically. "Everybody knew how fond you were of your mother, my lord. I think the fact that you came to your father's defence by giving that testimony persuaded the jury, not the testimony itself."

For a moment both were silent and Miss Nerts was going over the details of the affair in her mind. It started ten years ago, when Lord N., who was already then a prominent politician and one of the most influential nobles of the North started an extramarital affair with a woman thirty years his junior. He wasn't the first man to cheat on his wife, no doubt, but Lord N. didn't even take the trouble to conceal his liason.

His elder sons were both married at that time and lived separately, and his youngest son, Alex, who was much younger than his brothers, was still at school. He was only sixteen at that time. Then there was a party where Lord and Lady N. and their youngest boy went to all together, and Lady N. drank a glass of wine and fell dead to the floor.

Lord N. was arrested on murder charges and the case looked grim for him, even though they couldn't find any poison present in his wife's body. Still the case looked clear enough and the motive was obvious. The prosecution insisted that the poison was put into the wine glass by the husband, and then Lord Alex suddenly came up with the testimony that he had drunk out of the wine glass first, hence the wine couldn't have been meddled with.

The jury was impressed by him defending his father. Lord N. was found not guilty and soon after the process was over married his mistress. His youngest son studied at a university at that time. Several months after his father's wedding he disappeared and nobody ever found out what had happened to him. Until Miss Nerts got her suspicions and went to the library to check old newspapers. And now he was sitting in front of her, in a dimly lit living-room, but even in that light she could see how pale his face was. He was staring into space with unseeing eyes.

Finally he came back out of his contemplation. "Yes, my interference was quite a success, wasn't it?" he said sarcastically. "After all, not only I saved my father's life, but also was instrumental to his consequent marital happiness, thought it hasn't resulted in any children."

"It was a heavy blow to him when you disappeared, Lord Alex," said Miss Nerts.

"Oh, I believe, he got over it eventually," replied Lennart. "He never took much interest in me, anyway. Harry was always his favorite. It didn't prevent him from climbing the career ladder further, in any case."

Miss Nerts sighed. "You hate him, don't you?"

"I have every right to, I suppose," said Lennart dryly.

"But think of what your father went through."

Lennart's eyes flashed and it was evident that he had difficulty in controlling his temper. "Am I supposed to feel pity for him?" he asked indignantly. "Have you asked yourself what I went through? Working in construction fourteen hours a day in a blazing sun, then dodging death rays in the jungles of Aargh?"

"Something tells me that you enjoyed the experiences, at least partly," said Miss Nerts calmly. "Am I wrong, Lord Alex?"

Lennart thought her words over and was too honest to deny the truth contained in them. His anger subsided. "You are an astute woman," he said. "Yes, I guess you are right. There were ups and downs in my life, but I probably wouldn't want it any other way."

"Why did you choose Aargh?" inquired Miss Nerts. "Why not the Baron Confederation?"

"You see, I wanted to go some place where nobody knew me, nobody would ask any questions and nobody would care whether I lived or died because at that moment of my life I didn't care about it myself, or so I thought. When it came to it, I found out I'd rather stay alive," replied Lennart. "I simply realized that our life is what we make out of it and proceeded to do my best."

"But you still won't forgive your father? You were just a boy when it happened; but now, when you became a man can't you understand him? He wasn't the first man to fall prey to a scheming woman," said Miss Nerts.

"Oh, I do understand him to a degree," answered Lennart coldly, "though I can't say I approve of his taste. Still, I understand that after more than twenty five years of married life he got tired of my mother, who had been nearly of the same age. I understand that he started an affair with another, not even trying to hide it from his own children. What I can neither understand nor forgive is that he murdered my mother to marry that gold-digging witch!"

Miss Nerts looked at Lennart, moved by the passion of his last words.

"He gave her all my mother's jewels," continued Lennart, unable to stop. "I had to sit at one table with her and listen to her vulgar conversation, and answer her politely. At one point she even tried to flirt with me. It was worse than all I had endured at school during my father's process."

"That's why you decided to leave?" asked the old lady.

"I decided to leave," said Lennart slowly, "because I realized that if I stayed in my father's house one day longer I'd kill both of them. That's why." An emotional outburst was totally untypical for him, and Lennart leaned against the back of the chair. He felt exhausted and empty inside.

"Poor boy," sighed Miss Nerts. "So you are sure that your father commited the murder, aren't you?" Lennart looked at her in astonishment.

"Of course," he said, "could there be any doubt? Who else could have done it?"

"Your father with all his drawbacks is an intelligent man," said Miss Nerts, "a politician. Had he really wanted to get rid of your mother, don't you think he could have found a better way? He should have known he would be the first suspect, and I don't think he counted on you defending him."

Lennart was bewildered. "You think it's possible that it was somebody else's work? But what motive would they have?"

"To get rid of your father, for instance," replied Miss Nerts. "As a politician, he must have a lot of enemies. Why didn't you ask him?"

"I had no desire to listen to another of his lies," said Lennart dryly. He regained his self-control and his face had its usual expression, cold and unemotional. "You may be right, Miss Nerts, for all I know, but it's too late for both of us. It's better to maintain the status quo; my father will stay a prominent politician, me a soldier of fortune. I have given up all my rights to an inheritance and found peace and I only hope he can feel the same."

He stood up and Miss Nerts followed his example. She understood by his tone that the conversation was over. "You are leaving tomorrow, aren't you?" she asked. "I heard you met a man called Mr Thompson who got interested in your business enterprise?"

"You know him too?" inquired Lennart.

Miss Nerts smiled. "Yes, but not under that name. He is actually my third cousin. I won't ask you what he wanted from you, but I'll give you some advice: be careful, and don't throw your life away. May the Lord bless you, Lord Alex."

Lennart was deeply moved by those words. He took her hand in his, kissed it and went out without speaking.

Chapter 6. Meeting an Old Friend

It took Lennart a couple of months to complete all the formalities necessary to start a business. His idea was to take the managerial functions for himself which meant that he had to study bookkeeping and many other things; on the other hand, he tried to improve his flying and navigating skills. As a retired officer he was given a possibility to train for getting a Class A pilot license.

The doctor who had treated him was content with the improvement of his general health. "I have always stated that native climate does wonders," he declared and proceeded to give Lennart the permission to get his flying hours. Only when sitting inside the craft again, Lennart realized how he had missed the experience. He came to the conclusion that he loved flying. His body seemed to react properly, but the doctor still shook his head. "You should never fly long distance alone," he advised. "It's too much of a strain." However, Lennart completed the training course successfully, passed the examinations, and got his Class A license. It had to be renewed after five years but he didn't look so far into the future.

The time not taken by flying was spent in studying economics, and then Lennart had to buy a ship and to complete all the paperwork, but finally, after four months, his company became a reality. He decided to call it "Drianon" as a reference to the place where his flying career started, his reasoning being that had Brian not deserted, his life would probably have taken a much different course.

By this time Brendan Stewart joined him. He seemed to become more cheerful, life on Aargh was quite different from Delta, and Brendan was thrilled with the new experiences. Lennart congratulated himself on his strategy working. He took Brendan to a couple of nice places where one could watch beautiful dancing girls by means of distraction, and hoped it would show his friend that the world did not end because one woman had rejected him. There were many others, better than her.

Here Lennart failed, though, as Brendan watched the girls rather gloomily and then stood up and left, declaring to his friend that he couldn't approve of the inhumane exploitation of women. Lennart could only shrug his shoulders, he didn't think that dancing girls on Aargh were exploited any more than in other places, but he knew it was impossible to change his friend's mind. He had to leave Brendan to himself as there were other things to keep him busy; besides searching for clients and establishing his business Lennart had to meet with a certain Mr Smith, a representative of Mr Thompson.

Mr Smith was a man of uncertain age, dressed in a gray business suit. He had gray eyes and graying hair as well. His lips were thin, and Lennart felt antipathy for him at the first sight. He was sure it was mutual. Lennart never came to know Smith's real name or rank, but when the latter opened his mouth, it was only to give orders; Smith didn't tolerate any talking back. Lennart felt nothing for being bossed around again, but there was little he could do about it. After all, he had agreed to work for the intelligence of his own free will.

Smith gave him a sheet of paper. "Here is the list of necessary equipment," he said. "Study it, Captain. This will be your first freight to Volcan. There you will be met by an agent of mine by the name of Amman; he will give you further instructions."

Lennart read the list attentively and nodded.

"One more thing," continued Smith, coldly. "Your partner, Stewart, has been drinking again, I heard."

"Only moderately," said Lennart. "By the way, what has it to do with the whole business?"

"A lot," said Smith. "It's your responsibility, Captain, to ensure that he behaves decently."

"What are you going to do if he doesn't, shoot him?" asked Lennart. He was irritated by Smith's tone.

"Not him, you," answered Smith dryly.

Lennart looked at him trying to understand if Smith was speaking seriously, and decided that he was. "You surely can't expect me to control my friend's behavior?" he inquired.

"I expect you to control your tongue in his presence, Captain," was the answer. "We have to maintain strict secrecy if we wish for the operation to be successful. Stewart is an unstable type who cannot be trusted. Do I speak clear enough?"

"Yes, sir," said Lennart, in his mind sending Smith to Hell. He was furious, but controlled himself. Smith was not a man to be trifled with.

The trip to Volcan was a three day journey, and it was the first long distance flight Lennart undertook with his new ship which he christened *Fortune*. He bought it from an acquaintance of his, a smuggler, who had assured him that it was the best of its kind; and so far Lennart was content with his purchase.

Brendan functioned as the first pilot and Lennart assisted him as the second pilot. The trip was rather uneventful, and Lennart's thoughts were concentrated on the details of the operation. Officially, they were transporting a party of weapons ordered by a Volcanian company called "The Desert Treasure", whose representative by the name of Amman was to meet them at the havens.

Lennart had told Brendan that much, and the latter didn't ask any questions. Brendan was a good pilot, but not a businessman, and he was perfectly content to leave all the financial issues and paperwork to his friend.

There were other things which Lennart dwelt upon. Volcan was the planet where, as he strongly suspected, Brian Alistair found an asylum, and that meant that Eileen, the slave girl, was probably there, too. While being on Delta and enjoying Margaret's company, Lennart had nearly forgotten about her, but the moment he heard the word "Volcan", his thoughts naturally turned to the blue-eyed girl who had risked her life to save his.

"I must be losing my mind," thought Lennart. "I'll probably never see her again. And even if I will, what then?" However, despite the indisputable logic of this conclusion, he kept thinking about the pretty slave.

Volcan was an economically underdeveloped planet with a tropical climate, rich in natural resources. It didn't have a central government, but was divided into several territories, controlled by competing tribes. They were independent in name only, as the more powerful neighbors of Volcan exercised a lot of influence over the local authorities, which as a rule were rather ineffective and corrupt.

As usual, the two chief rivals were Delta and Uranius. The part of Volcan where Lennart had to go was called D'har, and it was in Delta's sphere of influence. The capital of D'har was Aranipor, and there were the headquarters of several Deltan companies exploiting the mineral rich mines of D'har mountains. There were also several factories built by Deltans producing mining and agricultural equipment. Lennart knew he could look forward to cooperation from the local administration.

Upon their arrival, they had to go through the customs and Lennart was looking through his papers, rather nervously, though he knew that they were in order. Everything was legal, but still, with the locals you never knew.

For both him and Brendan it was the first visit to Volcan. Lennart was accustomed to a warm climate, but in the city of Aargh where he lived, it was rather dry, while in Aranipor the climate was both hot and humid. The space haven building looked shabby and didn't have air-conditioning and Lennart had to wipe the sweat dripping from his forehead. They had to wait for quite some time until one of customs officials appeared to deal with them.

He was a short, fat, balding man in his mid-forties, and looked like a person of mixed parentage, half Aarghean, half Volcani. He was dressed in a white shirt and khaki pants, and had a handkerchief in his hand which he used to wipe his face. He introduced himself as D'haki, and Lennart expected that he would have to answer a lot of questions, show his papers and let the ship be searched, but instead D'haki shook hands with him and Brendan, signed the papers and informed him that a representative of "The Desert Treasure" waited for them outside.

He accompanied the two friends to the exit and Lennart saw a figure dressed in white standing there. There was something familiar about the man. He was looking outside, into the street, but then turned his head and looked at the group who were approaching him. At that moment Lennart finally recognized him.

"Brian," he shouted, "Brian! Well I never!" and forgetting all the dignity ran to his friend and they embraced. "Boy, am I glad to see you again!" exclaimed Lennart. "Brent, this is Brian, the friend of mine I told you about."

Brian smiled. "The name is actually Ben Amman," he corrected his friend. "A citizen of Volcan and an employee of 'The Desert Treasure'." He looked at Lennart significantly, and the latter checked himself.

"I knew you went to Volcan, but I never thought you'd find a decent employment," he said. "It was a wise desicion to acquire Volcanian nationality. I hope you are happy over here."

"Perfectly," smiled Brian. "You have made acquaintance with mister D'haki, of course, but he probably didn't inform you that he is our business partner, did you, D'haki?"

"No," said the customs official. He was speaking Westen with a curious accent. "I thought I'd wait till they meet you. Gentlemen, you will be staying in my house. I have some things to do and will join you later, but Mr Amman will escort you there."

Lennart was still bewildered at the turn the events were taking, and he was eager to talk to Brian alone. Brendan probably sensed the two had things to discuss, and very soon upon arriving at D'haki's house left them, under the pretext of feeling tired.

The house was a spacious villa with a lot of rooms and plenty of servants. D'haki was obviously a rich man. Yet, as it was often the case on Volcan, the unrefined luxury was combined with the lack of the most elementary things. Air-conditioning there wasn't installed, either, though in the living-room a big fan was working. Lennart sighed and comforted himself with the thought that at least there were modern bathrooms, a refrigerator and a color TV.

"I never expected to meet you here, Brian," he said. "That was a surprise, if ever. I wonder why Smith told me nothing about it."

"He probably had his reasons for it, as he has for everything else he does," answered Brian with a grimace which showed what he thought of Smith. "By the way, I have to thank you, I guess."

"Oh, you mean that incident a year ago?" asked Lennart. "So I was not mistaken, it was you. And the girl must have been Eileen. Why did you object to my seeing her face so much?"

"Because I had to play the role," said Brian. "Volcanis are terribly hung up about such things, you know. And then I wasn't sure whether you recognized us and what would be your reaction if you did."

"You surely didn't think I'd betray you?" inquired Lennart indignantly. "Anyway, what happened to you afterwards?" He felt strange reluctance to ask directly about Eileen.

"You were otherwise pretty mad at me when we parted," reminded him Brian. "As to what happened, well, I came to Volcan and met D'haki who helped me to get the legal status. And then I was made an offer I couldn't refuse. So now I'm an independent contractor in the service of Delta."

"You work on your own, then?" asked Lennart, surprised. "They didn't offer you a position as an officer?"

"Me, a renegade twice sentenced to death?" said Brian bitterly. "No, they didn't extend such a courtesy to me."

"I see," said Lennart. "And the girl, what happened to her?"

"You will see her soon, probably," answered Brian.

"Is she here, in this house?"

"She will soon become the mistress of this house," informed him Brian. Lennart looked at him in astonishment. "What do you mean?"

"It's better that you know it right away, probably," replied Brian. "She is engaged to be married to our host. You see, when I came here I had nothing left, but her. D'haki liked her and promised to help with papers if I sold her to him. I refused initially, but he kept insisting. Finally I agreed. He fell in love with the girl and decided to marry her. That's all."

Lennart became angry, he didn't know why. "You'd sell your own mother if the price were good," he said. "How could you do it to her?"

"D'haki treats her decently. He is a rich man, and she will be provided for. That's more than I could give her," answered Brian.

"But he is a half-caste."

"And she is a slave. She can't count on anybody better than him," said Brian. "By the way, why such interest for her fate? I remember you didn't want to take her when you got your chance."

"You know I couldn't take her with me," retorted Lennart. "She risked her life for me, and naturally I feel concerned."

"I don't think it's natural at all, after more than a year," said Brian. "Anyway, the fact is that she is D'haki's fiancee and keep in mind that when you meet her, you should behave accordingly."

"How did she become a slave?" asked Lennart. "I bet she comes from a good family."

"She does," replied Brian, "but she fell in love with a man her father didn't approve of and decided to elope with him. He then proceeded to sell her as a slave. That's all."

"I see," said Lennart.

They were sitting on the verandah and the sun was going down before their eyes. Lennart felt strangely sad, he didn't know why but that story touched him deeply. He didn't want Brian to guess his feelings, and so he changed the subject and started talking about business matters.

Chapter 7. The Wedding

That evening they spent with D'haki, eating, drinking and watching a couple of girls dance, but Eileen didn't appear. Lennart knew he shouldn't drink too much as his anti-fever medication wouldn't work, but D'haki kept proposing toasts and Lennart thought it would be impolite to refuse.

He kept an eye on his Deltan friend, who seemed to forget all the promises he had made; wine was flowing, the dance was getting more sensual, one of the girls, a dark-haired, dark-eyed Volcanian beauty dressed in clothes made of sheer fabric showed an obvious interest in Brendan. Her movements were gracious, the gold bracelets and necklaces she wore were tinkling, her mouth was half-open, showing perfect white teeth, and there was desire in her eyes.

She came very close and made snake-like movements and it was more than Brendan Stewart could bear. He looked at Lennart, and the latter nodded. Soon his friend disappeared with the girl, and the two other dancers turned to Brian and Lennart. Lennart chose a light-skinned, auburn-haired one, and he wouldn't admit it even to himself that the reason was that she reminded him of Eileen.

When he woke up next morning the sun was already rising and the temperature in his bedroom was close to +30°C. The girl was gone and Lennart had but a vague remembrance of her, and a splitting headache. He had a slight hope that it was just a hangover, and not an attack of esquai, but when he tried to get out of bed, the room started swirling around him and he had difficulty in keeping on his feet.

He got to the bathroom somehow, but washing his face in cold water didn't seem to help, and he had nothing else to do but to get back to bed. In fact he nearly collapsed on the floor before he could reach it. Lennart wasn't sure how late it was, but apparently they missed him at breakfast and sent someone to check. He thought that the door opened and closed, and then after some time it opened again and Brian went in.

He looked at his friend's face, took his hand and checked the pulse and shook his head. "I won't ask you how you feel," he said, and then proceeded to give Lennart a glass of water and the medicine. "Drink this and try to get some sleep," he advised. "You'll feel better in a couple of hours. I'll see if I can send somebody to stay with you in case you need anything." After this he left the room thinking by himself that his friend was in for it, for a couple of days at least.

The medicine worked, though not immediately, but finally Lennart was able to fall asleep, and when he opened his eyes he couldn't understand at first where he was and what exactly happened. The sun was getting down and the room was dark, with a small lamp burning, and there was somebody sitting by his bed. Lennart shook his head trying to focus his eyes. The pain and fever were gone, but he felt light as a feather. The figure moved and bent over him. "Are you feeling better, Captain?"

The voice was familiar, and then he saw her face and recognized her. It was Eileen, dressed all in black, with her hair totally covered by a black scarf, but she wore no veil and he could see her face. There was a worried expression in her eyes.

"I think I am," said Lennart. "What happened to me? And what time is it?"

"9 p.m. standard time," she answered, "and you got an attack of esquai. It seems now to be over, thank God. Do you need anything?"

"A glass of water, please," asked her Lennart.

He sat up in his bed and found out that he was still feeling dizzy, and also very hungry. She came back with a full glass in her hand and gave it to him, and their fingers touched each other. Hers were trembling lightly. Her eyes avoided his; she looked down at his chest. Lennart had taken off his pajama jacket, or may be he had forgotten to put it on last night, he didn't remember any more, and she suddenly blushed.

Lennart had well-developed muscles due to constant training and he could be called quite handsome were it not for the scars on his chest and left arm and shoulder. She turned her eyes away. Lennart drank the water and put the empty glass on the table by his bed, then made a sudden movement and caught her hand in his. "Eileen," he called and she turned and looked at him, and when he saw her eyes he knew that she loved him.

For a moment he forgot where he was and that the woman in front of him was engaged to another man. For a moment the world around him stopped existing and there were only the two of them, and nothing else, but that moment didn't last long. She freed her hand and took a step back. There was silence for a moment, and when she finally spoke, it was evident to Lennart that she had difficulty in controlling her voice.

"Do you need anything else, Captain?" That question sent Lennart back to Earth, or rather to Volcan, and he remembered everything Brian had told him. The dream disappeared. The woman who stood before him was not a beautiful princess, she was a former slave engaged to her master, in whose house he was, and he had to respect it.

"I think I am hungry," he said, and she nodded.

"I will give orders to bring you dinner, and after you have eaten it, you should take your medicine and get back to bed."

"I'll take a shower first," said Lennart. "Will you help me to get out of bed, Eileen?"

She looked at him and there was a twinkle in her eyes. "If you keep your hands to yourself, Captain."

"I promise I will," said Lennart and he did.

She stayed with him until he fell asleep again and then quietly left the room, and as she turned and looked at him sleeping peacefully, there were tears in her eyes.

The next day Lennart felt much better, but Brian who came to visit him in the morning, insisted that he spend one more day in bed. "It's for your own good," he said. "By the way, how did you like the nurse I sent you?"

"She was excellent," said Lennart, "but I haven't seen her today yet."

"I'm afraid she has other things to do," replied Brian. "Her wedding is in three days, and we are all invited, even your Deltan friend, who, by the way, spent the whole day yesterday drinking. It seems he suffers from remorse because he betrayed his moral principles, or something to the point, I'm not sure."

"I don't give a darn about him," said Lennart. "He always finds a reason to drink. Tell me about Eileen. Does she really have to marry that guy? She doesn't love him!"

Brian shook his head. "Love has very little to do with it," he said, "and we both know it. Get her out of your head, Len, seriously. It won't lead to any good for both of you."

Lennart had to admit his friend was right, but when three days later he had to witness the wedding ceremony all his good intentions to forget her disappeared, and the one thing which was left was the intense desire to possess her. The thought that she officially belonged to another drove him mad.

D'haki was a rich and influential man, and the head of his clan, and the villa was full of guests. There was beating of the drums, and wild music, and dancing, and plenty of food, and the atmosphere of excitement in general. After the traditional toast to the gods the newlywed couple finally left, and following an old ritual the guests went with them till the bedroom door and wished them all the happiness in the world.

Lennart, who was still feeling far from well, became even paler than he had been, when the door closed. He understood it was just a formality, as

Eileen had belonged to D'haki before, but then she had been a slave, one could buy her. Now she was a free woman and D'haki's wife, and unless he divorced her, which was unlikely, she was lost to Lennart forever.

"You look pale as a vampire," said Brian, taking his friend by the arm and dragging him away. "Try to control yourself. Think what happens if somebody else knows."

"You should have never sold her to D'haki," said Lennart. "I'm sure this marriage will be unhappy."

"It will be quite happy if you don't interfere," answered his friend. "By the way, I must inform you that the punishment for adultery on Volcan is death by stoning, for both the adulterer and the adulteress. I have seen it done once, and let me tell you, it's a very unpleasant way to die. If you don't care for yourself, think of her. And D'haki is our most important ally, too. We can't afford to lose his good will. Forget her, Len, please. That's the best you can do."

"I was not planning to commit adultery," said Lennart dryly. "And if I want to listen to a sermon, I'll go to church instead."

"I have never seen you attend one when on Aargh," remarked Brian.

"It's because I didn't care for the religion they practice over there," retorted Lennart. "Nevertheless, I have some idea of morality, strange though it may seem to you. It includes the notion of adultery being a mortal sin."

"I thought fornication was one as well, but that never seemed to stop you before," said Brian sarcastically. "You just steer clear of the girl, Len, and I mean it. Promise me that you will."

Lennart cursed instead of an answer, and went outside. He stood on the verandah and thought Brian's words over. Of course, Brian was right, and he had been behaving ridiculously. Even if Eileen were free, he could never marry her. And then there was Margaret, waiting for him on Delta. He took a decision and went back to search for Brian. He had to forget Eileen and he would do it, too.

Chapter 8. The Microchips

It was easier said than done as during the next several months business regularly brought Lennart to D'haki's house, where he couldn't avoid meeting Eileen. He kept his promise to Brian to leave her alone, and always kept the distance, treating her with utmost formality, and she responded in the same manner, but her eyes betrayed her every time.

It was a painful situation for both since they seemed to be doomed to spend a considerable amount of time in each other's company. Luckily, her husband didn't suspect anything; and always met his guest cordially, which made it all the worse for Lennart.

He had to pretend he shared the friendly feelings when deep in his heart he harbored totally different emotions. In fact, sometimes he felt he could kill D'haki. The thought of Eileen, with her elegance and fragile beauty sharing bed with him was enough to drive one crazy, and to add insult to injury Lennart had to listen to D'haki's bragging about what for treasure his young wife was.

He managed to control himself though, but often caught Brian staring at him in the peculiar manner though the latter never referred to Eileen or Lennart's feelings any more. Brian knew his friend better than anybody else and was perfectly aware that Lennart had quite a temper which he usually concealed under cold reserve, and that it was better not to provoke him too much.

Meanwhile Lennart didn't have much time to dwell upon his disappointment as running the company was more work than he had ever expected. He had other clients and orders besides his activities on behalf of the government of Delta, and Brendan proved to be of not much help. In fact, Lennart became more and more pessimistic about his friend's future. Brendan seemed to become more indifferent to life around him every day, and to sink into his own world, and what was the reason behind it, Lennart could not comprehend.

He himself had an active mind and his ambition drove him to achievement. At the moment, Lennart was obsessed with the desire to make "Drianon" highly profitable, so that he not only could exist without Deltan government contracts, but also become wealthy, and with that objective in mind, he tried his hand at the stock market speculations. Lennart had an insight and a sense for business, but he missed the theoretical knowledge and thus spent every free minute studying.

The rest of his energy was used to smuggle weapons to Volcan, where Brian was responsible for transporting them further to Tarna. Aargh was a big weapons producer and exporter, but some weapons fell into the category of forbidden to export, or there were quotas on how much one company could export in a year. Lennart, driven by Smith's incessant demands estimated that in one year he violated more rules than somebody else would in ten, but such was his luck or skill that he had never been caught so far.

It was easy for him to conceal his illegal activities from his friend, because Brendan never bothered to check the books and didn't ask many questions, but too much work started taking toll on Lennart's health. In a year's time he had but one short vacation which he spent with Brendan on Delta where he again was confronted with his old problem; should he propose to Margaret or not.

She was still in love with him and didn't try to conceal her affection, and he came to conclusion that he liked her very much, too; though the feelings he had for her were very different from those he had for Eileen. Eilen was lost to him, however; but he knew he could have Margaret if he wished to.

Common sense prevented him from declaring these feelings as Lennart realized only too well that his own future was rather uncertain. He went back to Aargh still undecided. Upon his return he had a meeting with Smith. They still disliked each other intensely, as in the beginning; and Smith kept telling him he should find a way to get rid of Brent, and Lennart kept finding reasons why he couldn't.

That time Smith had a longer face than usual, and Lennart soon found out why. There had been information leaking, and Uranius was busy with preparing a counteroffensive.

"You should be exceedingly cautious, Captain," warned him Smith. "The enemy is probably watching your every move. They won't dare to attack on Aargh, but on Volcan anything can happen. There soon will be the election of the new governor in D'har, and the pro-Uranius party is getting stronger by the day."

After communicating this information, Smith, as usual, gave Lennart a list of weapons that were needed, and upon reading it Lennart shook his head.

"The microchips you are asking me to get are forbidden for export. The new technology, which is kept a secret, is used for their production. Why the need for such sophisticated weapons?"

"It's none of your business, Captain," said Smith. "The question is, can you get them for us?"

"I'm not sure," said Lennart. "The risk is too high. If they catch me with that stuff on board, the future will look grim for me."

"Nevertheless, we need them," declared Smith sharply. "They are a part of a new anti-air defence system, and can be used by the Tarnian autonomy to protect themselves from air strikes by Uranius, in case they support the rebels."

"I will try," replied Lennart. "I'll do my best."

"You'd better," said Smith and rose, showing that the conversation was over. As it was often the case Lennart for a moment was possessed by a strong desire to break Smith's neck, but upon thinking it over decided against it.

He succeeded in obtaining the microchips, and everything went fine, against all his expectations. Lennart wasn't superstitious, but a strong feeling of doom seized him. Something told him he might run out of luck this time.

They were more than half way through their journey when Lennart got a headache. He had been straining himself all the last time, and the matter of the microchips weighed heavily upon his mind. The pain got worse and worse and finally he couldn't take it any more and had to leave the bridge contrary to his own wishes as he didn't care to leave Brendan alone.

Last time they were on Delta, Brendan heard that Elinor had got a son, and that event threw him into a new fit of depression. He had been silent nearly all the time of their trip and kept staring in front of himself with unseeing eyes.

"Brent, keep an eye on things, will you?" asked Lennart. "I'll go and lie down for half an hour."

"It's OK with me," said Brendan rather indifferently.

Lennart went into his compartment, took three pills instead of one prescribed and collapsed upon his bed with a groan. It took him much longer than half an hour to recover; in fact, the pills made him drowsy and he fell asleep. When he awoke, he had a strange feeling in his stomach, and soon realized what was the reason of it: the ship was shaking and making strange maneuvers.

With a curse Lennart got upon his feet and went to the bridge, and the picture which he saw took his breath away. There was no one to steer the ship, as his first pilot lay drunk upon the floor with an empty bottle of whisky in his right hand. The autopilot wasn't turned on, either, and the ship was heading right into an asteroid field.

For a moment, Lennart totally lost it. He remembered all the curses he had ever heard on Aargh, and addressed them to his careless friend, though he could have talked to a wall with just as much effect.

There was no time to lose, however, and Lennart controlled himself, suppressed the strong desire to kick the figure on the floor, and taking the first pilot's chair proceeded to set the ship back on its course. Lennart wasn't a good navigator and the task was not easy, as the ship had been left unmanned for a couple of hours at least, but finally he succeeded.

In five hours they would be landing on Volcan. Lennart left Brent on the floor, and there he was lying still, muttering in his sleep, when they finally had to land. The *Fortune* was a large ship, and it was a lot of work to land her properly, and now Lennart had to do it all alone, while suffering from both the effects of his recent breakdown and the drugs he had taken.

He heaved a sigh of relief when he finally managed to do it but his misfortunes were not over yet. Some half way through his landing maneuvers Brendan came back to life and was now sitting next to him, looking quite miserable. He didn't talk and Lennart didn't say one word to him, either. He was still quite mad, and his desicion was taken. Brendan had to leave the company.

"I'll take a loan in the bank to pay him off," thought Lennart, "but whatever it costs me, it can't go on like this any more. After all, I'm not running a charity. This time he has gone too far."

Normally when they arrived at Volcan, they were met by D'haki himself and the customs control was a mere formality, but not that time. D'haki was nowhere to be seen and instead of him, there were two other officials, and they didn't look particularly friendly. Lennart as the ship captain was taken aside and had to answer all sorts of questions, and then they searched both him and Brent and started to search the ship, using a military scanner.

Lennart knew what they were looking for, but thought that he had to express indignation and demand an explanation. He was informed that it was a routine control, and they were checking all the ships arriving from Aargh for illegal drugs. The explanation was ridiculous, since most drugs on Volcan were legal anyway, but there was nothing Lennart could do about the whole thing.

"What does it mean?" whispered Brendan. "What are they searching for?"

"How do I know," said Lennart shrugging his shoulders. He wiped the sweat from his forehead for the ninth time in a row, but that didn't surprise anyone as the day was exceptionally hot, even for Aranipor.

Finally, the scanning team came back, evidently disappointed. "You may unload your cargo, Captain," said one of the officials, and signed the papers. Lennart's face relaxed just a little bit. Outside they were met by Brian, who appeared more than a little anxious.

"I have been worrying about you both," he said, looking at Lennart significantly. "Did everything go fine?"

"It did," said Lennart, deciding that the confrontation with Brendan could be delayed. "Why didn't D'haki come?"

Brian looked around. "Somebody informed the officials that a huge party of illegal weapons was expected to be smuggled to Volcan from Aargh. Coincidentally, D'haki had to go away on some business. They have been searching all the ships from the early morning."

"Luckily for us, we don't carry anything illegal," said Lennart. "Tell your men they can start unloading. I'll give them directions myself."

"I'd say you'd better go to bed," remarked Brian sympathetically. "You do look ghastly. Anything the matter?"

"Just one of my headaches," said Lennart. "I'll get over it, but I want to oversee unloading personally."

He turned and addressed Brendan who had been avoiding looking him in the eyes ever since they left the ship. "Brent, you'd better go to D'haki's house and inform Mrs D'haki that we arrived. She must be worried by now."

It sounded more like an order than a friendly suggestion, and Brendan nodded and disappeared. The stevedore crew of "The Desert Treasure" was already waiting for them at the dock. Lennart went inside the cargo area, followed by Brian; touched a panel to the left and it opened into an empty space where a small box was hidden, which he took out and gave to his friend.

"I'll always be infinitely thankful to the guy who sold that ship to me," he said, "and now let's get out of here as soon as possible. I won't feel safe until we are in D'haki's house."

When they arrived there, Eileen was waiting for them and she was visibly anxious and upset. She looked at Lennart's face, pale and worn out and turned away. "Your friend told me you had trouble with customs, Captain," she said in her melodious voice.

"It was nothing to worry about," lied Lennart, "just a routine check up. By the way, where is Brendan?"

"He left and didn't say where he was going," replied Eileen.

"That just takes the cake," exclaimed Lennart, and told Brian about all his troubles, not caring much for using gentlemanly expressions.

They were sitting on the low sofa in the living-room, their feet sinking in the carpet. The fan was working at full capacity, but the room still reminded Lennart of a sauna.

"I have warned you from the very beginning," said Brian, "that this Stewart character is a good-for-nothing. And Mr Smith shares my opinion, too. What are you planning to do now?"

"I don't know," answered Lennart gloomily. "He invested a lot of money into that company. I can't buy him out without going into debt. And then, I'm losing a pilot."

"That's just too bad," agreed Brian.

At that moment, the living-room door opened and one of D'haki's manservants rushed in, gesticulating wildly. He was speaking Westen mixed with a Volcanian dialect which Lennart couldn't understand, but Brian interrogated him in his own language and his face became very sober. He turned to Lennart and said, "Your friend has just been kidnapped."

Chapter 9. A Difficult Decision

Lennart who had a cup of coffee in his hand nearly dropped it to the floor, splashing the hot beverage on his knees. He cursed and jumped to his feet, putting the cup on the side table. "Just how exactly did it happen?" he asked the servant. "Speak." The man looked first at Lennart, then at Brian, and started talking rapidly in his own language.

"His Westen is not that good, I'm afraid," said Brian casually. "Volcanian basic education still leaves much to be desired." Lennart had an idea about Volcanian basic education, but refrained from expressing it. "Can you interpret his words?" he asked instead.

"Sure," replied Brian. He started asking the servant questions, and then turned to Lennart who had seated himself back on the sofa. "He says that he had the night out and went to town, a couple of hours earlier this evening. When he was coming out of a bar he saw your friend walking along the street. He was walking rather uncertainly, as if not sure which way to go. Suddenly, a black all terrain with tinted glass in all the windows stopped in front of him and a man came out, dressed in a business suit. Jashur says the man started asking something, and Stewart was answering him, when the second guy came out; he was looking like a bodyguard: black pants, black shirt, and sunglasses. He evidently had a weapon in his hand, which he shoved into Stewart's ribs and that argument worked so well that Stewart went along with him. They pushed him into the car, onto the back seat, and the bodyguard went with him. The business type took the driver's seat and they left. It all happened very quickly, probably within a couple of minutes. Jashur was on the other side of the street, standing between two houses, and luckily they didn't pay attention to him. When the car disappeared, he ran the whole way back. That's all."

"Did he notice the license plates?" asked Lennart.

"He looked, but it seems there was mud all over them."

"Which direction did the car go?"

Brian started talking to the servant again, and then replied: "In the direction of the center, but of course, they could go anywhere. Do you want to know anything else?"

"I've heard enough," said Lennart.

Brian sent the man away with orders to bring more coffee and both friends looked at each other. "And D'haki is still not home," remarked Brian. The servant entered the room with a tray in his hands, served them coffee and announced, "Supper ready."

"Later," said Brian dismissing him and turned to Lennart.

"They probably followed him from the Havens and have been watching this house for Heaven knows how long. Of course, we went by car with a couple of security agents with us, but he was an easy target. I should have known —."

"No, I should have known," interrupted him Lennart. "It's all my fault. I have dragged him into this whole business, and used him as a tool, without ever warning him of the risk he was taking. I'll never forgive myself. His death will be on my conscience."

"You shouldn't blame yourself, Len," Brian tried to comfort him. "How could you know it'd come to this? Anyway, why couldn't Stewart just stay in the house and wait for us? Apart from this whole espionage business, the suburbs of Aranipor aren't safe at this time of the day. He should have known it. There is one positive side to this whole story: Stewart knows nothing and thus can't betray us. It would be much worse if me or you were in his place."

"Do you realize what you are talking about?" asked Lennart. "You understand they'll torture him and then kill, do you? They are probably torturing him now, while we are drinking coffee over here."

"Most probably they are still on the way to wherever they are taking him," said Brian, "but when it comes to torture, the one who know nothing says nothing."

"We must rescue him," stated Lennart decisively.

"Rescue him, how?" inquired Brian. "Do you know where they took him? Do you have a plan? In any case, we should wait till D'haki comes home; he has his own men with the local police, and probably can find out who is behind it. We'd better eat now, and then you should go to bed and rest, at least for a couple of hours, otherwise you'll be good for nothing tomorrow."

Lennart realized that Brian was right, as he was close to exhaustion. He thought he wouldn't be able to sleep, but when he lay down he fell asleep almost immediately. When he opened his eyes the sun was shining through the window, and the air was fresh and cool, as the temperature suddenly dropped at night, as it sometimes happened over there. It was a beautiful morning, but Lennart had a nasty feeling inside him and suddenly he remembered everything that had happened the day before. It took him only a couple of minutes to pull on a pair of trousers and a shirt, and then he went to search for Brian whom he found in the breakfast room, as he had expected.

"You didn't wake me up, when D'haki came back, as you had promised," he said reproachfully.

"You needed rest more than anything," said Brian in response. "Now sit down and take a crescent roll, our hostess baked them with her own dainty hands, specially on the occasion of your visit. She is a treasure of a woman, Mrs D'haki, isn't she?"

"I can't eat until I know what's going on," insisted Lennart. "Did D'haki find out who's behind the kidnapping?"

"Let me tell you a story," suggested Brian. "You have probably heard from our friend Smith about the election of the governor, which is going to take place soon? Basically there are two local families who will fight for the position. One family stands firmly on guard of Deltan interests, and D'haki's clan is a part of it. The other one, well, you guessed it—there is Uranius behind them, but besides this fact, there is simply clan strife between the two, and they hate each other. The pro-Uranians hold a lot of power in the Western part of the province, among various desert people, while D'haki and his relatives control Aranipor, but not for hundred percent, as you noticed yesterday. Stewart's kidnapping was just another move in that eternal strife, and presumably your unlucky friend was taken to the compound of the Uinur clan, which is situated more than 300 kilometers to the south-west of the city of Aranipor, in Araki desert. There is a trade route from Aranipor which goes through the desert to the western parts of D'har, and the car which answers the description given by Jashur was seen on it last evening, just before the sunset. The compound lies on the outskirts of Be-na-zi Mountains and can be described as a stronghold. D'haki has no real power or authority in these wild parts, and thus I'm afraid there is nothing we can do about the whole situation."

Brian finished his story, leaned on the back of his chair and took another crescent roll. He always had a good appetite in the morning. Lennart poured himself a cup of coffee. He was thinking his friend's words over and there was silence in the room for quite a time.

Finally, Lennart spoke. "I'm going there," he declared. "Right after breakfast."

"No, you are not," said Brian. "You are mad."

"I'm the one responsible and I won't leave Brent to his fate," insisted Lennart.

"How exactly are you planning to rescue him?" inquired Brian. "What if they take you prisoner? Are you sure you can withstand torture? You'll ruin us all!"

"All you care about is politics," retorted Lennart. "I care about my friend's fate. I don't want to live with his blood upon my hands."

"And I heard Stewart has a pretty sister, too," remarked Brian. "She apparently also figures in your decision, doesn't she? Wherever you go there always seems to be some skirt attached to you."

"Leave Margaret out of it," said Lennart, and his eyes flashed dangerously. "She has nothing to do with the whole business. I'm not asking you to accompany me, but don't try to stop me, either."

"Do you realize what Smith will do to you when he learns about this whole affair?" asked Brian.

"The hell I care," was the answer.

Brian looked at his friend attentively and sighed. He knew that Lennart was stubborn and when he once took his decision, he would stand by it.

"You are crazy, you really are," he said. "And I must be crazy as well because instead of tying you by hands and feet and locking you up in the cellar I'm helping you, but there is nothing else I can do, I'm afraid. I'm going with you, Len."

Chapter 10. The Rescue Operation

"We need your help," said Lennart. The three of them; he, Brian and D'haki were sitting in D'haki's home office with a detailed map of the disctrict in front of them. It was still early in the morning, but the sun was high enough for it to be unbearably hot. Their host sighed.

"I'm afraid there is not much I can do," he said. "We have no control over that territory, and we cannot storm the compound. It will lead to an open war between the clans and nobody wants it."

Brian looked at his friend with "I have told you so" expression on his face, but Lennart was unmoved. "I wasn't planning to storm it," he announced. "I had something else in mind." Brian became interested for the first time.

"Care to tell us what it is?"

"Patience," said Lennart. "You'll learn everything in a couple of minutes. Mister D'haki, as I understand you have here some sort of a disease prevention service, don't you? The one which must ensure that no epidemies occur."

"Yes," answered D'haki looking rather surprised.

"And you could make an announcement on the radio declaring that a dangerous epidemy broke out somewhere, say close to the Be-na-zi mountain chain and everybody needs to get vaccinated in order to survive?" continued Lennart. "Make it something really scary, like I don't know...."

"Black Death," suggested Brian who thought that he started understanding his friend's intentions.

"I was thinking about anthrax or some similar disease," replied Lennart. "It must be deadly enough, you know."

"Well," said D'haki slowly, "suppose I do what you are asking me, Captain, what then?"

"Then you just have it repeated a couple of times," explained Lennart, "in between regular programming on short waves, together with traffic information and weather reports, but the radio announcer shouldn't know where the information comes from; so that if investigation is conducted later, it couldn't be traced to you directly. And then we will need an ambulance, and a small group of volunteers, and a certain amount of vaccine, that's all. Oh yes, and the protective costumes, of course."

D'haki still looked as if he didn't fully comprehend Lennart's plan.

"He wants to use this disinformation in order to be allowed to enter the compound," explained Brian.

"Brilliant," said Lennart. "You are making a quick progress today."

"Why would you want to vaccinate your enemies against anthrax or whatever disease?" inquired D'haki. "Besides they must know you by face and will recognize you."

"Not if we are wearing surgeon masks and goggles," responded Lennart. "And I'm not going to vaccinate them against any disease; I'm planning to use a strong sleeping solution instead. And when they fall asleep, we search the compound, find our friend and disappear. Of course, we will also need some fake ID's, I nearly forgot about them. Nobody dies, there is no bloodshed, and hence no reason for the war between the clans, and I doubt there will be an official complaint, either; and if there is, you just state that you know nothing about the whole affair. The fake ID's are burned, together with the costumes, the ambulance gets a new coat of paint and license plates, and the announcement on the radio was just somebody's stupid joke. Those responsible for broadcasting it got fired, that's all."

D'haki looked at Lennart with something like admiration in his eyes. "You will get what you need, Captain," he declared.

D'haki could, if necessary, act really quickly and it took him less than a couple of hours to provide the two friends with what they needed. Lennart got a small bus and four of D'haki's men as a support group. One of them functioned as a driver, as he knew the territory really well. Lennart and Brian sat next to him in the cabin, while the other three were inside the bus where they had all the necessary equipment to represent a disinfecting team. They had to spray a powder which supposedly killed the bacteria, but was in fact just the substance used by Volcanis to brush their teeth; by reason of their country being less developed they still didn't switch to toothpaste completely.

The road was practically empty as the route was chiefly used by night when the temperatures were easier to bear; and those who carried on trade with mountain tribes always travelled as one big group instead of many scattered trucks due to safety reasons.

The compound was further than a three hour trip away and when they left for it, the sun climbed more than half way to zenith, and the temperature inside their bus was close to 45°C. "It will likely get worse," sighed Brian.

As an exception to the general rule, their vehicle had air-conditioning installed but by some reason it didn't work properly. They had a big supply of water and it helped to some degree, but Lennart still didn't find their journey a particularly pleasant experience.

The epidemy warning was repeated several times, and Lennart hoped that by the time they'd arrive to their destination everybody in the neighbourhood would have heard it. The view outside the windows wasn't cheerful in the least, but the mountains got closer and closer. When it seemed that they wouldn't be able to tolerate the heat for much longer, the cooling system finally started working, and they could breathe normally again. The rest of the way they spent discussing the details of the operation.

"Brian, you'll have to do all the talking," instructed him Lennart. "You speak Volcanian, I don't. Try to sound as authoritative as possible, because our success chiefly depends on whether we can convince them to believe our story and cooperate or not. So officially you are the leader. Tell D'haki's men not to engage in any discussions, and to use their eyes while they are spreading their stuff. If they find anything suspicious, they must report as soon as possible. It's really unfortunate we couldn't have the modern costumes with built-in radios, but got those rags instead." Lennart looked at his own costume of a gray-greenish color with loose-fitting wide pants and a long loose jacket which reminded him oversized pajamas, with disgust.

"Be glad that you got them at all," was Brian's answer. "D'haki wasn't really enthusiast about helping us, as you may have noticed, and those jackets are really good if you carry concealed weapons. By the way, you should keep your cap on the whole time, as there aren't many blond Volcanis, you know. Neither do a lot of them have blue eyes."

"That's why I thought goggles were essential," grinned Lennart. "So while D'haki's guys are spraying their tooth powder, we just go inside and vaccinate everybody, and use this as an opportunity to search the compound as well. Then after half an hour they all fall asleep, we search the compound more thoroughly, hopefully find what we seek and then disappear. D'haki was positive they'll sleep for several hours at least, so when they finally wake up we are back home."

"And what then?" inquired Brian. "I mean, what are you going to do with the company and all that?"

"First things first," replied Lennart. "Let's find Stewart, and then we'll see."

The compound looked like a fortress, and the walls around it were about five meters high, the heavy gates were closed, and there was nobody to be seen, but Lennart got an uneasy feeling that they were watched. The bus stopped in front of the gate, and Brian went out and knocked at the door which was next to the gate and evidently meant for pedestrians.

A small window in the upper part of it opened and Lennart heard a rough voice apparently inquiring what their business was. Brian started speaking in Volcanian and then showed his identification card. Their ID's represented them all as the employees of the government department of prevention of dangerous diseases and looked official enough.

The guard apparently wasn't initially convinced, but the demonstration of the card settled the question and the gate was opened. They drove into the yard and parked their bus close to a truck. There were several other vehicles in the parking place, but none answered the description of the car used for kidnapping.

They all went out, D'haki's guys carrying their equipment. The driver had to stay inside and wait for them. Lennart looked at the house in front of him. It was one story high, but had a basement and an attic and looked big enough to host fifty people if necessary.

A mean-looking Volcanian came out of the house and it was evident that he was an authority figure. He came close to them, followed by two bodyguards, and they weren't looking friendly. The man who had opened the gate for them, stood close to the group, listening. Brian looked at Lennart as if asking for moral support, then faced the men and started telling his story. Lennart knew enough Volcanian to get a general meaning of what he was saying.

"There is an anthrax epidemy in your neighborhood," stated Brian and then added something incomprehensible. Then Lennart could catch the words: "did you listen to the radio today?" The mean-looking man was evidently pondering the problem, he looked at Brian's ID, then turned to Lennart and demanded to see his, then asked, "What exactly do you want?"

"We are conducting a vaccination campaign," said Brian solemnly. "The only way to stop the spread of the deadly disease is to vaccinate against it. My men will also spray disinfencting powder in the living quarters of the building."

"Will it take long?" asked the man, and upon hearing that it couldn't possibly take more than half an hour, nodded and allowed them to proceed.

Brian looked at Lennart significantly. "My assistant here will give each of you an injection while I'm going to make a list of all vaccinated adults." The man looked instantly suspicious.

"Why is it necessary?" he inquired.

"For the government report," declared Brian, opened a briefcase he was carrying, took an officialy looking file out of it and addressed the man again: "Your name, sir."

"You can write me down as T'hun," stated the man.

"You are going to be vaccinated first, because you are more important," informed him Brian and nodded to Lennart. "Just roll up your sleeve on your right arm."

While Lennart carried on vaccinating, Brian, after writing down the names of three others, started a long story about anthrax and the dangers of it. He described the disease in such convincing details that Lennart began to feel rather uncomfortable and wonder if he had any symptoms himself, even though he had been vaccinated against it while serving the Republic of Aargh. The disinfecting crew left, and one of the guards went with them to show them about, but T'hun stated that there was nobody else in the house.

"Women have to be vaccinated as well," informed him Brian. "Are you sure there are no women in the house?"

"This place is used as the winter residence of my master, mister Arkos," said T'hun. "In summer he doesn't spend much time over here. We are the only inhabitants, and there are no women."

"Fine," said Brian and turned to Lennart who had finished his business and was looking around with interest. He did notice a barrel of a small laser canon on the roof and thought that there were probably more.

"Go inside the house," ordered Brian, "and check the work of the disinfection crew. Tell them to hurry up, we need to visit some villages to the West of this place and the time is short."

Lennart nodded and went into the house. He checked room after room, but there was nothing particular to draw his attention. D'haki's men were busy spraying and the whole house was covered with white powder which nearly made Lennart sneeze. He found the guard sitting on a chair in one of the rooms, looking very sleepy. He was a youngster of about eighteen and apparently didn't need much to fall asleep.

Lennart told the men to keep on spraying until he came back, and asked himself where he should go first, to the basement or to the attic. His sixth sense told him that the basement was the most probable place for keeping a prisoner, and so he descended the stairs and found himself in a dimly lit corridor with doors on both sides.

There was no one to be seen and the doors were mostly closed. There were seven on one side and six on the other, and only two opened when he pushed them. Lennart took out a flashlight he had carried in his pocket and briefly searched the rooms, but there was nothing to be seen, they both were filled with rags and old junk. He started knocking on other doors and calling, but there was no answer.

Lennart hesitated. Should he go to the attic, or may be back and wait until everybody is asleep, and then they could search the whole house thoroughly together with Brian? At that moment he heard a noise behind one of the doors, and then something reminding a groan. Lennart knocked lightly and called Stewart by his name and the groan repeated, louder than before.

The door was locked, but gave way when Lennart kicked it in, and he found himself in a small room without any light. Lennart switched on his flashlight and there on the cement floor he saw something which first reminded him a heap of old clothes; but then it moved and groaned again and Lennart realized it was his friend. He knelt before him and when he saw Stewart's face he started swearing.

"Brent, do you hear me?" he called, and the ghastly figure opened his eyes and stared at him. "It's me, Lennart," he continued tearing away his mask and goggles. "Don't you recognize me?"

Before he could get an answer to his question, he heard a strange noise behind him and his quick reaction was what saved his life. There was a man standing in the open doorway with a raygun in his hand, ready to shoot.

Lennart had no time to pull his out and did the only thing he could throwing the heavy flashlight into the man's face. He apparently didn't expect it and nearly lost his balance firing somewhere into the ceiling. The next moment Lennart was at him; he didn't intend to kill his enemy as he had promised to D'haki there would be no victims, but he soon regretted it: the man was stronger and though Lennart forced him to drop his gun to the floor, he soon realized that he was fighting for his life.

His enemy was heavier as well, and with his weight he was now pinning Lennart to the ground while with one hand trying to grab the gun back. Lennart managed to kick the weapon with his foot and it flew into a corner of the room, his adversary cursed and for a moment got distracted; and Lennart, realizing that this was probably his last chance, gathered all his strength, pushed the man aside and jumped back to his feet.

His enemy was still on his knees and before he could recover Lennart kicked him hard into his face, and then again and again; suddenly he saw the man collapse and watched as if in a slow motion picture as the lifeless body was falling to the ground. Lennart didn't need to check his pulse to know that his adversary was dead as he had evidently kicked him against his temple.

Chapter 11. The Trip to Fern

"Well, I guess it couldn't be helped," said Brian philosophically. "The question is, what shall we do now? D'haki won't be pleased when he knows."

"We should dispose of the body," told him Lennart. "On the way here I saw a couple of dried up wells, we can throw it into one of them. Or we could burn him, and then throw what remains into a well. That will at least partly cover up what happened."

"I don't think so," returned Brian. "They did fall for our anthrax story but they are not total idiots. There is a hole in the ceiling as well."

"So what?" asked Lennart. "It doesn't prove anything. Anyway, it's still better than leaving him over here. And we have a long way before us, so let's get moving. The sooner we get back to Aranipor, the better. I'm afraid Brent won't make it."

"Bastards," said Brian. "You know, if not for D'haki, I'd kill them all in their sleep, without any remorse, either. I'm glad you got at least one of them. By the way, are you not hurt?"

"I'm OK," replied Lennart.

In reality his left arm felt numb as it always did when he strained it too much, but he didn't think the fact was worth mentioning. Both Stewart and the corpse were taken away and placed inside the bus, and before leaving the basement, Lennart checked if there were no traces left. They dragged the three inhabitants of the compound who were sound asleep into the house so as not to leave them lying in the sun, and started their journey back.

D'haki's men were superstitious and didn't like sitting close to a dead body; they apparently got the idea that his death would bring them bad luck. Apart from their murmuring the way back was totally uneventful. Lennart and Brian after some consideration decided not to burn the body as smoke could attract attention, and just dumped it into an empty well. It was very deep and Lennart hoped it would provide a good hiding place. Brendan was unconscious when they brought him to D'haki's house, but he was still alive.

"I think we could better take him to the hospital right away," declared Lennart, but D'haki shook his head.

"The fewer people who know about what happened, the better," he stated and Brian agreed with him.

"I think Stewart will be OK," he said. "He was severely beaten and will surely need dental work, but with good care, he will recover soon enough."

After a brief examination they found out that Brendan had likely a couple of broken ribs, missed his front teeth, and his whole body was covered with bruises, but there was no worse damage to be seen.

"We came just on time," was Brian's opinion, and Lennart agreed. Thus his unlucky business partner was trusted to the cares of Eileen, and the two friends went back to D'haki's office. Their host looked sober when he heard about the death of one of the inhabitants of the compound, but said nothing, only nodded. They ate their dinner and then Lennart, who was very tired and had pain in his arm, excused himself and went to bed. The next day he slept till late and was woken up by Brian, who brought him coffee.

"It's 11 a.m. standard time," he said, "I thought there was a Deltan proverb about early to bed early to rise and such."

"There is," agreed Lennart, "but I couldn't fall asleep till rather late."

"I see," said Brian and became silent. Lennart looked at his friend's face and realized something was wrong. Brian was apparently hesitating, but finally started speaking.

"Have you ever asked yourself how the weapons get to Tarna, Len?"

"I guess that you deliver them there, through your company," replied Lennart.

"One of Tarna's moons is inhabited, too, as you probably know," said Brian.

"Yes, of course, you are speaking of Fern, aren't you?"

"Fern is an independent state, which is not officially under the power of Uranius, even though they have a peace treaty which places a lot of restrictions upon them; for instance, they are prohibited from having a strong army and are under an obligation to cooperate with Uranian authorities," continued Brian. "So the weapons are shipped to Fern and from Fern further on, to the Tarnian autonomy, then they are smuggled over the border to the occupied territories. Officially though, 'The Desert Treasure' ships carry no weapons on board, but the parts of agricultural machinery produced here on Volcan. You get my point?"

"Why are you telling me all this?" asked Lennart, surprised.

"I'm in a difficult situation," replied Brian. "I had to leave today with a cargo for Fern, but there is information that Uranians patrol the route, searching random ships. My pilot is local and superstitious as most of them are. He keeps talking about ill omens and stuff and says he has two wives and seven children. He positively refused to fly. And to crown it all, something happened to the engine of my ship and I suspect it's sabotage. There is an information leak and it looks as if one of D'haki's men works for the enemy."

"In other words, you need a ship and a pilot," summed up Lennart.

"I feel like I have no right to ask you," sighed Brian. "The risk is huge, but otherwise I'm not sure what I can do about the situation. I have my schedule to follow and D'haki doesn't like having those microchips in his house."

"Fair is fair," said Lennart finishing his coffee and getting out of bed. "You went with me yesterday and I'll go with you today. Had I known it from the beginning," he added, "it could have saved us the trouble of unloading the ship as now we have to load it up again."

"I'll pay you for it," suggested Brian, but Lennart declined.

"I'm not doing it for money. On the other hand, it's better to do it as officially as possible so that I sign an official contract with your company to deliver the agricultural machinery parts to Fern."

"I'll fix it," promised Brian. He looked much more cheerful. "It's now a quarter after 11, I think that in less than five hours we can leave."

Fern was at a distance which required a four day journey with a normal sub-light speed; "warp" speed wasn't normally used for such short distances as it required precise calculations and an enormous amount of fuel. The first couple of days all was quiet and Lennart started thinking by himself that they would make it without any problems.

He chose a route which went through an uninhabited part of Sector X, it was longer than a normal trade route, but he thought that they were probably least expected there. On the third day they both sat on the bridge playing cards as the *Fortune* was steered by the autopilot, when suddenly Lennart looked up and saw the enemy appearing out of nowhere. There were five Uranian light cruisers, flying in a combat formation. It was no use trying to escape, and he knew it. Brian looked up too, and his face suddenly got a gray tint. The radio spoke.

"You have entered the Uranian zone of influence. Military authorities have the right to search any ship. You have ten minutes to decide your course of action. If you decline, you'll be destroyed."

Lennart and Brian looked at each other.

"I knew it would end like this," said Brian. "If we refuse, they'll destroy us; and if we allow them to search the ship, they'll find it is full of weapons while on paper we are carrying the reserve parts of tractors! Do you understand what it means? We are toast. At least, as an officer you can be exchanged, but they'll do a search on me, and then...." He didn't finish his sentence.

"Why do you think they would exchange me?" inquired Lennart. "Such as I are a dime a dozen, especially taking into consideration the fact that the operation will utterly fail. We'll go down together."

"At least, if we surrender, it'll give you a small chance to survive," insisted Brian.

Lennart thought for a moment.

"If I'm to die, I'd rather die fighting," he stated finally, "and I think we have a chance."

"If we attack them, it will be pure suicide," said Brian.

"No, it won't," objected Lennart. "We can pretend that we are attacking them, then switch to warp speed and disappear. I think we have enough fuel for that."

"Fuel may be enough, but I'm not so sure about your navigation skills," remarked Brian. "If you make but a small mistake in your calcualtions we'll collide with some asteroid and that will be the end of it."

"I think I'll take that risk," said Lennart. "I need a place for maneuvers and some time. Man the canon, and try to cause as much damage as possible. Fire at my command."

The radio spoke again. "Ten minutes are over. Have you taken your decision?"

"Yes, I have," said Lennart slowly. "You may go to Hell!"

Chapter 12. Lennart and Jinescu

While speaking, Lennart pulled a joystick towards himself and sent the ship into a breathtaking maneuver which nobody could have expected it to be able to perform, turning it with its nose towards the enemy and at the same moment both Brian and Uranians started firing. The ship was shaking and Lennart could only hope that the protective shields which he had recently installed were really as good as described by the advertisment, which stated that they could withstand a direct hit with a large caliber laser canon.

He soon found out that the smuggler who had sold the shields to him didn't lie, as the *Fortune* shook from top to bottom but no worse damage happened. "We lost two shields," shouted Brian. "We have only two more left, and then they'll get us, hurry up!"

Lennart did his best, but it wasn't an easy task to calculate his route through hyperspace with the enemy firing, the ship shaking, and himself trying to outmaneuver better trained Uranian pilots. Suddenly Brian uttered a scream of joy. "I got him," he shouted, "I got him!" There was a flash and one of the enemy cruisers was no more.

Nearly at the same moment Lennart finished his calculations and pressed the button. He half expected there would be a bang and the world would end for him, however, after what seemed an eternity, the darkness around disappeared and the stars were shining again, there was no trace of the enemy to be seen; instead, right in front of them, there was Fern, the place of their destination. They had done it!

Lennart turned very slowly and looked at Brian. He was in some sort of stupor, still unable to believe that they had managed to escape, and his friend seemed to feel the same way. "Brian," he said, "go to the bar and check if Stewart left anything, will you?" Brian obeyed and came back with a bottle of brandy and two glasses. He poured one for himself and one for Lennart, and his hands were shaking so much that half was spilled to the floor.

"To me and you," said Lennart, "and to our success, down the hatch!" The brandy warmed him up and he felt better.

"We did it!" shouted Brian, "you are a genius, Len!" He started dancing a wild dance and Lennart joined him. They drank the rest of the bottle which was not much, considering that Brendan Stewart had found it before them, and then broke it by throwing it against the wall.

They spent three days on Fern as the *Fortune* needed some repairing done. Two shields were lost and the other two were not an adequate defence, so that Lennart would have to buy new ones upon returning to Aargh. Brian insisted on paying all the expenses, and Lennart didn't object. He had formed a plan and asked his friend if he would like to become his business partner, instead of Stewart. However, Brian wasn't really enthusiast about it at first.

"You aren't a very experienced pilot, Len, and I'm even worse; and besides, don't forget that I can't show my face on Aargh."

"More than two years have passed," shrugged Lennart his shoulders. "I bet they are not looking for you any more. Your personal presence on Aargh is also hardly necessary. You will be my partner on paper, and get the dividends; as for the pilot, I'll hire one of D'haki's men. I just don't want to take another loan from the bank, you see, and I know you made good money with 'The Desert Treasure'."

"I'll think of it," promised Brian. "First, let's get back to Volcan."

It was easier said than done as Lennart soon found out. This time Uranians were with seven ships including a heavy cruiser, and they were completely surrounded and warned that any wrong movement on their part would lead to instant annihilation. Lennart didn't doubt that the enemy spoke the truth; the first time their attack was totally unexpected and it gave them a chance, but it wouldn't work the second time.

On the other hand, there was no smuggleware on the ship and the papers were in order, so that he still had some hope, but not very much. Anyway, their only chance was to surrender and try their luck once again.

The Uranians took over the *Fortune* and started searching it; while both friends, handcuffed, their weapons taken away from them, under heavy escort were transported to an Uranian cruiser where they were to be interrogated personally by the officer in charge of the whole operation, whose name was Jinescu, and who had a rank of lieutenant-colonel.

Jinescu was a man of about forty-two years old, of an average height, with black hair, dark eyes, and a very unfriendly expression on his face. His eyes were cold and piercing, and there was a smile on his thin lips when he first looked at his prisoners. Neither Lennart nor Brian tried to resist or protest as it was totally useless, until they were brought to *Sando*, which was the cruiser's name, but now Lennart thought it was time for him to say something. After all, a completely innocent person would certainly be indignant at such treatment, which was against the international law as well.

"I demand an explanation," he stated looking right into the Uranian's eyes. He tried to feign his most innocent face expression as well.

"You are not in a position to demand anything," said Jinescu coldly. "You are here to answer my questions, and you'd better answer them to my satisfaction, do you understand?"

He spoke Westen with the peculiar accent typical for Uranians.

"You have no right," started Lennart again, but at that moment one of the guards hit him with the rifle butt on his stomach, and for some time Lennart lost the ability to breathe and think coherently. Jinescu patiently waited till his prisoner stopped coughing, and then inquired: "do you have any more questions?" Lennart, still unable to speak, only shook his head.

Brian had the face of a person whose death sentence had been already signed and Lennart understood that from this quarter no help would come. He would be the one to do all the lying. He hoped that at least Brian would have enough good sense to follow his story and give the correct answers.

Jinescu looked from one to the other and then asked: "Which one of you is the ship's captain?"

"I am," said Lennart.

"Your name, age and nationality?" inquired the Uranian.

"Lennart Duncan, twenty seven, Aarghean," answered Lennart.

Jinescu looked at the confiscated ship papers lying in front of him on the table, then again at Lennart. "You don't look like an Aarghean," he stated and added something in a language Lennart thought was Tarnian.

"I'm sorry, but I don't understand," he said. "As for my not looking like an Aarghean...my father was a businessman from Delta."

"So you were not born a citizen of the Republic of Aargh?" was the next question.

"I got my citizenship through army service," answered Lennart.

Jinescu seemed interested and started asking questions about Lennart's military career. "So you took part in the operation 'Dawn of Hope'?" he asked and Lennart had to answer positively, though he was sure that Jinescu wouldn't like him more because of it.

"Well, at least you are honest," said the Uranian. "What was the reason you left the army?"

"I was honorably discharged because of my injuries," explained Lennart.

"What exactly is wrong with you?" asked Jinescu.

"I think they call it a 'Veteran syndrome', though it has a longer scientific name, among other things," replied Lennart, "which made me unfit for active service, or something to the point."

"And yet you function as a pilot," remarked Jinescu. "How can you explain this, Captain Duncan?"

"I needed to earn a living somehow," said Lennart. "The pension I got from the Republic wasn't enough to cover my needs, so I started a business, which is, by the way, perfectly legal. Besides, may be you'll find it strange, but I simply like flying."

"Oh no, I don't," assured him Jinescu. "According to the documents, your second pilot is a certain Stewart, born on Delta, is that him?" he pointed to Brian.

"No," said Lennart. "Stewart got suddenly sick and had to be substituted."

"Then your name is evidently Amman, according to the passport you were carrying," said Jinescu addressing Brian, who nodded in response as he was obviously unable to say a word. "Nationality Volcanian, and if these papers are to be believed, you are the owner of 'The Desert Treasure', the company which sells agricultural machinery produced on Aargh, is it correct?" Brian nodded again.

"Can you speak?" inquired the Uranian.

"He speaks Westen very bad," said Lennart, "but he understands everything. His mother was an Aarghean, so we speak this language to each other." Brian nodded one more time.

"Tell me about your business," ordered Jinescu, and Lennart started a long tedious story which was so boring that the lieutenant-colonel was not able to listen to the end of it. He waved his hand in the air. "Enough already, Captain. Yours is a perfectly legal business, I got it."

"I want to know what I'm accused of," demanded Lennart.

"Four days ago a ship very much like yours attacked and destroyed one of our light cruisers," said Jinescu, looking at Lennart's face attentively. "All the crew perished. What can you say to this, Captain?"

"That I'm very sorry," said Lennart. "As for my ship, there were many of the same type produced on Aargh ten years ago."

"That's true," agreed Jinescu. "My lieutenant tells me you got a canon on board, why?"

"Have you heard about pirates?" asked Lennart.

"I'd like to know more about your flying career, Captain," said the Uranian. "Tell me about it, from the very beginning, where and when you learned to pilot a craft, how many years you functioned as a pilot, etc etc."

Lennart obeyed and proceeded to tell him about his experience as a pilot. Jinescu thought a bit, then looked at Brian again. "And that gentleman, I see, has only a class B license."

"That's true," said Lennart, "but as I have told you, my partner got sick and I took him as an assistant, which is quite logical, as I was contracted to deliver the cargo to one of his usual clients because his own ship had suffered some technical problems."

At that moment, a young lieutenant entered Jinescu's office and started talking in Uranian. Jinescu listened attentively, asked a couple of questions, then dismissed him and sank into some sort of a contemplation. He finally arose and looked at both prisoners.

"I just got a report of the team which had searched your ship, Captain," he said slowly. "There was nothing illegal found."

"It's because my business —." started Lennart.

"Is perfectly legal, I know," interrupted him Jinescu. "Well, it seems that there is nothing else left for us to do but to believe your story, Captain. I must apologize for having detained you in this manner."

"It's all right," assured him Lennart. Brian made some strange sound and nodded again.

Jinescu gave an order to one of the guards and their handcuffs were removed, the ship documents were returned to Lennart, and the friends were escorted back to the *Fortune.* Lennart still couldn't believe they got off so easily, but the Uranian war ships switched to warp speed and disappeared, and they were left alone. At that moment Lennart did something which he hadn't done for many years. He got down upon his knees and thanked Heaven for saving their lives.

"Why do you think they let us go?" inquired Brian, who finally got his tongue back.

"They were not impressed by my qualifications as a pilot," explained Lennart and they both laughed.

Chapter 13. D'haki

If it depended on me, I'd have you court-martialed," stated Smith.

"What for?" asked Lennart innocently.

"For disregarding orders, which could have had disastrous consequences."

"I didn't receive any orders on how to deal with the situation," said Lennart, "so I had to handle it myself. I was taught that showing initiative when necessary is one of the qualities of a good officer, you see."

"I see that you are incorrigible," sighed Smith. "You are going back to Delta and let Thompson deal with you as he sees fit, but not before you deliver another cargo to Volcan. You'll have to collect Stewart as well, as I understand."

"He was still recovering from his injuries so I deemed it better to leave him in D'haki's house for a while," explained Lennart.

"The decision to finally get rid of him was the only positive moment in this whole story," remarked Smith. "However, I'm not sure if Amman is the right substitute."

"What's wrong with him?" inquired Lennart. "I thought he was on our side."

"He is a renegade sentenced to death twice," declared Smith. "He is not on our side, he works for us as an independent contractor, do you see the difference, Captain?"

"Brian is a decent guy," protested Lennart. "He hasn't done anything that bad. He simply fought for his country's independence, that's only natural, isn't it? And concerning his second death sentence —."

"Yes, what about it?" interrupted him Smith. "Do I understand correctly, Captain, that you don't consider high treason anything really bad? One can commit it and still stay a decent guy? Is that your opinion?"

"No, of course not," said Lennart. "That's not what I meant. I simply want to say that I find it unfair —."

"What exactly do you find unfair, Captain?" asked Smith coldly, his gray eyes fixed on Lennart's face.

"Nothing," said Lennart. "Anyway, Amman hasn't agreed to my proposal yet."

"Well, it's not really my business," shrugged Smith his shoulders, "but if you get into trouble with him, Captain, remember that I have warned you about him. His true character may be not exactly as you think it to be."

"Darn," thought Lennart, "why must he always talk to me as if I were a schoolboy?" but aloud he said, "Yes, sir," with his usual reserve.

His second pilot was one of D'haki's men and Lennart was quite content with his choice. That time they got to their destination without any trouble, and weren't harassed by the customs, either. D'haki was absent, but they were met by his cousin who recently started working for the customs. The rumor went that D'haki would soon get a higher position in the administration of the region, and his cousin, a young man about Lennart's age by the name of Aghi, would take his place.

Lennart got his papers signed and went outside the building. He was surprised that Brian didn't come to meet him as usual, and didn't send anyone, either. He reached for his mobile to phone, but at that moment the familiar car stopped in front of him and he saw the driver and Brian next to him. His friend had a very peculiar face expression. He didn't get out of the car, but made a gesture inviting Lennart and his pilot to get in.

"What's going on?" inquired Lennart, stepping inside. "Why are you late and where is the working crew?"

"They'll come tomorrow," said Brian. He was speaking in Aarghean, as it was a habit between them. "As for your first question..." he paused for a long time and then continued: "there has been an assasination attempt. One of D'haki's bodyguards, Jadet. It happened a couple of hours ago, and nobody knows yet. I have always suspected that it was one of his own men who betrayed us."

Lennart needed some time to digest the information. "Do you mean to tell me that D'haki....That he is dead?" he finally asked.

"Not yet, but it won't take long any more," informed him Brian. "He is now in the hospital, with his wife. We are going there."

D'haki lay in a separate room, heavily guarded, and one look at his face was enough to convince Lennart that he wouldn't last long. Though unconscious, he was moaning in his agony. The doctor just left, and the only person present in the room besides him was his young wife. When the two friends entered, she stood up to greet them, her face was deathly pale and there were black circles under her eyes. She suddenly looked years older.

"It's very kind of you, gentlemen, to come here," she stated, her voice melodious as usual, and looked at Lennart briefly, then lowered her eyes. The whole way to hospital he was thinking about the implications of

D'haki's death. How many times he wished her free, but he never thought it would come in this manner, and now looking at D'haki he felt something very close to remorse.

"How is he?" inquired Brian, who appeared to be the only one unmoved. "What did the doctor say?"

"That he won't live another hour," answered Eileen and her voice trembled. "I only hope he will speak to me before he goes."

At that moment the dying man opened his eyes and muttered something incomprehensible. She sank to her knees clutching his hand in hers and started talking passionately in Volcanian. Lennart couldn't follow her words exactly, as she was speaking fast, but he got an impression she was apologizing for not being a good enough wife.

"Make an effort, my lord, please," she repeated, "don't leave me alone." Those words Lennart understood quite well and suddenly he realized that she experienced the same emotion as he did. She felt remorse for not being faithful to her husband in her thoughts. Suddenly D'haki spoke. "Jany," he repeated, "jany."

Lennart knew that it meant 'darling' in Volcanian. Those were the last words D'haki ever said as the next minute he was dead. Eileen turned to them and she had evident difficulty in speaking. "If you excuse me, gentlemen, I wish to stay alone with my husband."

"Yes, of course," they stammered together and left the room, the door closed and Lennart, who was the last leaving heard her sobbing hysterically. His first instinct was to go back and try to comfort her, but Brian grasped his wrist. "I don't think it's a good idea," he stated calmly. "Can't you wait at least until the funeral? By their tradition it will be tomorrow."

"You misunderstand me," said Lennart coldly, freeing his hand.

"I understand you better than you understand yourself," replied Brian, unmoved. "Let the women weep, we have other things to do. The traitor should not escape unpunished. I just got a message which says they traced him down to Sulaki, a suburb of Aranipor. A very disreputable place. A support group is on the way and I think we should meet them there."

"Fine idea," said Lennart.

They found their man in a tavern and when he saw that they were with eight people he didn't try to resist, but instead sank to his knees and started begging for mercy. It was such a pitiful show that Lennart didn't have the heart to shoot him or to order somebody else to do it. He looked at Brian uncertain about what to do. After all, Brian was in charge as D'haki's men obeyed him practically as they did their own master.

Brian had a disgusted expression on his face. "Take him out," he ordered, and it was done though their victim was wailing loudly and grabbing the furniture, all in vain.

"I have an idea," said Lennart, addressing his friend. "Let me fight him. It will be a better way to get rid of him."

"How typical of you," shrugged Brian his shoulders. "You are always a gentleman, Len, but you are probably right, though it's too much honor for him."

He announced his decision in Volcanian. The traitor became visibly agitated. He was quite good at fencing, as Lennart, having seen him demonstrate his skill more than once, perfectly well knew; but he was sure that he was still his superior.

Jadet had only a raygun with him, which they took away, but he had no sword, and Brian had to lend him his own. D'haki's men made a circle around them, so that nobody else could approach the duelers, and various visitors of the tavern who decided it was worth it to get out and watch could only do it from a distance.

Lennart's adversary was taller and heavier than him, but Lennart had an advantage of speed and a better technique, and exactly when Jadet least expected it he dealt the lethal blow. The polariton blade went half way through his chest and Lennart stepped aside quickly but still got blood upon his clothes. He looked at the lifeless body, lying on the ground and pushed it with his boot.

"That's the end awaiting every traitor," said Brian in Volcanian, but Lennart understood him and added "amen" to that. They left the body on the street and went back to D'haki's villa. "That was neatly done, Len," said Brian admiringly. "Now about other things. Your friend is much better, but he keeps to his room, doesn't talk much and is all the time sober. It seems to me he has learned his lesson. You are taking him back to Delta, aren't you?"

"Yes, I was planning to leave as soon as possible," answered Lennart absent-mindedly. "Preferably tomorrow."

"I have thought your proposal over, and I think I agree," proceeded Brian, "but first you'll have to settle it with Stewart, you know."

"I'll do it," promised Lennart. "Then I'll come back and arrange all the official matters on Aargh. You don't have to appear there in person, a proxy with legal powers to represent you will be enough."

“Was Smith mad at you?” inquired Brian, but Lennart only shook his head distractedly. “Not more than I had expected him to be. By the way, Brian, what will D’haki’s death mean to us? I want to say, for the business matters,” he corrected himself.

“Nothing will really change,” replied his friend. “D’haki’s next of kin will succeed him, he is a nice guy and totally on the side of Delta. You know him too, remember that youngish looking tall fellow by the name of Dessin Aminid?”

“No,” said Lennart, “not really. Do you think Eileen is still in the hospital? I think we have to inform her that her husband’s death is avenged.”

“It’s more appropriate if we wait until she returns home,” said Brian, “but if you insist....”

She was still in the hospital, and though her eyes were red and swollen from tears, she wasn’t crying any more. She looked cold and emotionless. Eileen listened to their narrative and nodded her head in comprehension.

“The justice was done,” finished Brian his story, as he was the one chiefly talking.

“Thank you,” was all she said, and there they left her. D’haki’s family who knew everything by now were all gathered in the hospital and she had to arrange the funeral.

“It was a long day,” sighed Lennart, sinking on the couch in the living-room which seemed so familiar and yet different. The sun had set behind the mountains. “I’d much appreciate something to drink.”

Chapter 14. Back to Delta

"I didn't have a chance to thank you before, so I'm doing it now," said Brendan Stewart. They just came back from the funeral and it was the first time that Lennart was alone with him.

"Listen, Brent," he started, "I think I have to explain something to you —."

"No, you don't," interrupted him Brendan with a faint smile. "Some things are better left unsaid. I only wish I hadn't caused you so much trouble. And not only you."

"If you mean D'haki's death, what happened to you has no relation to it," assured him Lennart.

"That's not exactly what I had in mind," replied his friend. "I just wanted to let you know how much I appreciate that you took such a risk only to save me, after all the stupid things I had done."

"I would never be able to look at myself in the mirror had I not rescued you," said Lennart, "and enough about it. I was just doing my duty, that's all."

"I hope that there will be no negative consequences for you," replied his friend, but Lennart only laughed in return. "I don't know what you are talking about, Brent. Tomorrow we are leaving for Delta with a regular passenger ship. *Fortune* has to undergo some repairs, Brian will see to it." He paused, unsure about how to announce his decision to Brendan in such a manner as not to hurt his feelings, but Stewart evidently anticipated it.

"After what happened you surely won't want me as your partner, will you?"

"Unfortunately, I don't think it's possible," stated Lennart. "When we get back to Delta, I'll write you a cheque for the whole sum of your investment, plus dividends. You can use this money for something else, you know."

"Yes, I know," said Brendan, his voice strangely indifferent. "Listen, Len, it's not necessary for my family to know what happened. I figured it's better to tell them I couldn't get accustomed to the climate."

"I think you are right," agreed Lennart.

All the way back to Delta he kept thinking about what he was going to tell Margaret. His decision was finally taken. Margaret was a sweet girl, but she deserved someone better than him. He couldn't offer her the kind of life she was accustomed to, his future was even more uncertain than before, and most important of all, Lennart finally realized that there was only one woman whom he truly loved and that woman was now free, and she loved him, too. It was everything that mattered to him, and since he couldn't have them both he made his choice.

Brendan Stewart didn't seem to pay much attention to his friend's state of mind; he was busy with reflections of his own, which judging by his face expression were of a serious kind. Mrs Stewart met them with her usual cordiality and Lennart felt ashamed that he had to lie to her, even though he knew it was done with noble intentions. Her mother's heart apparently told her that there was more to the story than what Lennart had told her, but she pretended to believe it.

Margaret looked rather disappointed. "Now Captain, you won't come and see us so often," she complained.

"I'm sorry," said Lennart. His consience was not totally clear, as he now understood that all the time he was giving her a reason to hope, when deep down he knew all along he didn't really love her.

Miss Nerts, who was invited on the occasion of their arrival, looked at Lennart's face attentively and didn't say anything. Theirs was not a cheerful company that evening and the next day Lennart had an appointment with Ferrash. He had told himself many times that he really had nothing to worry about, at least as long as the government of Delta needed his services, but the next morning when he was entering a certain gray building his heart was beating faster than usual.

Ferrash met him with a sober expression on his face. "Sit down, Captain," he said instead of a greeting. "I was just reading a report concerning your behavior, and the author of it has some very unpleasant things to say about you."

"I would guess so," replied Lennart gloomily. "He never could stand me, anyway."

"You are accused of insubordination, among other things," continued Ferrash. "And of acting contrary to instructions of your superiors, disregarding orders and putting the success of the whole operation in jeopardy to advance your own personal goals."

"I suppose my actions could be described in that manner," agreed Lennart. He suddenly felt tired and didn't even make an attempt to defend himself. "If that's their gratitude for my risking my neck for them all this time, so be it," he thought and looked at Ferrash with quiet resignation.

"Those are serious accusations," summed the colonel up. "Is there nothing you can say in your defence, Captain?"

"What would you do in my place, sir?" asked him Lennart.

There was something like a twinkle in Ferrash's eye. "We are not discussing my behavior, Captain," he said. "Answer my question."

"I would do it all over again," informed him Lennart defiantly. "That's the only thing I can say, sir."

"Well," said Ferrash, "I see that you are continuing to exhibit the same behavior which irritates our friend Smith so much, and it doesn't help your case. In the army one has to follow orders he gets, Captain."

"I was never given any orders," retorted Lennart. "I had to deal with the situation myself and I did what I considered my duty. If you think I deserve a punishment for this, so be it."

"I think you deserve a warning," said Ferrash. "A stern reprimand. See to it, that this doesn't happen again, Captain, because next time you won't get off so easily."

"Yes, sir," answered Lennart.

The colonel suddenly smiled, and his face got a warm expression. "It was an honorable thing to do, Captain Duncan, even though I can't approve of it. The risk was too high. Still I'd probably do the same thing myself. If I were your father I'd be proud of you. And your behavior when you were taken prisoner by Uranians was admirable. Now let's get back to business. The operation 'Liberation' is drawing to its end. There is still one big party of weapons which you are supposed to transport to Volcan. Amman is officially going to be your business partner as I understand, and I think it's only logical that you should assist him in delivering the weapons to their destination, Fern. As you know now, it was the task performed by one of D'haki's men, but after D'haki's death the new head of his clan doesn't want to get involved in it whether personally or by proxy. The enemy unfortunately learned too much due to Jadet's betrayal, and he considers that the risk is too high. There is, however, one more service I'm going to ask of you, Captain, and I want to warn you beforehand that it's a dangerous job and you have every right to refuse, in which case Amman will have to perform it alone or with any assistance he'll be able to get. I want you to ensure that the last transport safely arrives to Tarna and the weapons achieve their proper destination, and that after our transfer base on Fern closes, it won't be possible to directly trace the weapons back to us."

"Are you asking me to do it because you don't trust Amman?" inquired Lennart. "Or do you have any other reason, sir?"

"There have been problems on Fern as well," replied Ferrash, avoiding to give the direct answer, "and Amman demonstrated last time that he tends to break down under stress."

"Tarnians are his people," protested Lennart. "He will never consciously betray them."

"But we are not," stated Ferrash. "Enough of it, Captain, just tell me whether you take the job."

Lennart was silent for a moment, then turned to Ferrash. "Before I leave for Tarna, I want to ask you something, Colonel."

"Yes," said Ferrash, surprised. "What is it, Captain?"

"Should I not come back...." began Lennart, then broke off and started again, with a more resolute voice. "Should I die, I want you to tell my father...." he stopped again.

"What should I tell him?" inquired the colonel. Lennart seemed to have changed his mind.

"Nothing. Just tell him how it happened, that's all. And give him my medals. Here they are," he continued, taking a small parcel out of his pocket. "Will you do that for me?"

"I certainly will," assured him Ferrash.

The encounter with Margaret proved even more painful than Lennart had expected. They were together in the garden with Mrs Stewart evidently leaving them alone on purpose.

"Why do you always have to go?" she inquired, with her eyes full of tears.

"Margaret, try to understand," said Lennart. "There are things which are not in our power to change. I have to go. I can't tell you more, but believe me, that I'm speaking the truth. There is something else I have to tell you," he continued. "You should not wait for me, Margaret. We have no future together."

"Why?" she whispered.

"Because I can never give you all the things you deserve, Margaret. You need a husband who will dote on you, and a cosy home, and a life of comfort. I can't give you all this."

"I don't care," she protested. "I don't need comfort and all that. I could live without it. I would wait for you even if it took me years."

"I should have told it to you long ago," sighed Lennart. "I'm not sure whether you ever can forgive me. Margaret, there is another woman who I love."

The girl looked at him as if struck by lightning, then covered her face with her hands and ran inside. Lennart stayed alone in the dark, he didn't feel like going in and facing her mother, but he had to. Mrs Stewart was sitting in the living-room, her children nowhere to be seen, looking very unhappy, but if Lennart could see his own face he'd know that he looked even more so. She raised her eyes when Lennart entered and looked at him.

"I'm sorry," began Lennart, but she shook her head.

"You don't have to apologize, Captain. I understand. Margaret is too young to marry anyway. Miss Nerts just phoned. She wanted to know if you could drop by. She couldn't come tonight but she doesn't want to let you go without saying good-bye."

"I'll go there immediately," promised Lennart.

"So you are leaving tomorrow, Captain," said the old lady, pouring him a cup of tea. Lennart nodded. "You don't look especially cheerful," continued Miss Nerts. "Is it because of Margaret?"

"I'm afraid so," he replied. "I just had to explain to Miss Stewart that I could not possibly marry her. I feel myself a scoundrel. I should have told it to her long ago, you know, but until now I still thought our marriage a possibility."

"What made you change your mind?" inquired Miss Nerts curiously.

"Something tells me I won't live long," stated Lennart. "A man in such a position as I am has simply no right to ask a decent girl to wait for him. I wouldn't want to leave her a widow to raise my child on her own. She deserves something better than that, but I'm afraid she is too young to understand."

"Is this the only reason, Captain?" asked Miss Nerts.

"No," confessed Lennart. "I'm afraid not. I don't know why I'm telling you all this really, but you seem the only person who I could ever discuss it with. There is another woman. I thought she was lost to me forever, but the circumstances changed...." here he stopped.

Miss Nerts sighed. "Life is a strange thing," she remarked. "We can make all sorts of plans, but then something happens which turns them upside down."

"It's true," agreed Lennart. "I'm glad that you understand me."

"Yes, I think I do," replied Miss Nerts. "I will pray for your safe return home, Lord Alex."

"I don't have a home," said Lennart gloomily. "I don't know where I belong, on Aargh or on Delta, but I certainly will appreciate your prayers, madam. May be God will hear you, since I don't believe He listens to me any more."

"He always hears us when we pray sincerely," answered Miss Nerts. "You should try it, my lord, and you'll see that I'm speaking the truth."

"After all what I have done wrong, could there still be hope for me?" inquired Lennart.

"You should never lose hope, Captain," replied Miss Nerts.

"I'd better be going now," said Lennart rising to his feet. "I'll think about what you said, Miss Nerts."

"And I will say once again, may the Lord bless you, Lord Alex," answered Miss Nerts. And so they parted.

Part III.
TARNA

Chapter 1. Rivals

Back on Aargh Lennart had a lot of things to arrange. The apartment which he had shared with Stewart seemed strangely empty now, and he felt lonely for the first time in his life. Lennart promised Brendan that he would send him all his belongings by mail, and it took him some time to sort and pack them.

While going through his friend's things, Lennart found a pack of letters tied up with a ribbon, the address on the envelope definitely written by a female hand. "These must be from Elinor," he said to himself. "To think that all poor Brent's misfortunes came because of her. I wonder what he will do now."

His thoughts then naturally turned to his own situation. There was still some work he had to do on Aargh, but by the end of the month he would be going back to Volcan. Lennart had formed a plan and said to himself that if his lucky stars helped him again that last time, he'd come back to the same apartment with Eileen. Then it would become his real home, a place to return after all his wanderings, and he wouldn't feel lonely any more.

Strange enough, for the first time in his life Lennart was desperately longing not so much for a woman's love, but for her company. It was very un-Aarghean, but Lennart still had too much of a Deltan in him and on Delta women weren't only mothers of men's children, but also their companions.

Lennart had seen Eileen briefly as on his way from Delta he had to go to Volcan first to collect his ship and his new pilot. Brian had installed the new shields and the *Fortune* was again as good as new. Rheen, the new pilot, found accomodation in the office of Drianon, where he occupied a small room, nearly a big closet and at the same time functioned as a guard.

He also represented Brian's interests and Lennart soon arranged all the papers. Four weeks after his return to Aargh Lennart finally received instructions from Smith concerning the last stages of the operation "Liberation", which chiefly coincided with what he had already heard from Ferrash, and left for Volcan. Smith himself was planning to go to

Volcan and have a meeting with both Lennart and Brian before they left for Tarna.

The new chief of D'haki's clan was his younger brother by the name of Aminid D'haki; he had three wives and several children, both boys and girls. He was rather disappointed in his hopes as when D'haki's testament was read it appeared that he had left all his money and his house and servants to his young wife, making Eileen a very wealthy woman and a desirable party to marry, but three months of strict mourning were not over yet, so that she got no proposals as of now.

Brian had his own house in Aranipor, but he often used to stay with D'haki, whose death, however, made him think about different arrangements. It was considered very indecent for a single man to spend a night in the house of an unattached woman. As a solution to the problem, Brian suggested to Eileen that she should invite D'haki's old uncle and his wife to come and stay with her, which she did.

Eileen had a lot of cares since managing her late husband's business affairs fell now upon her shoulders, and though she proved capable and even shrewd, it was still too much for a woman, and thus she appreciated the old man's help and advice and his wife's company. Lennart and Brian spent some time discussing their plans, and then the conversation naturally switched to their pretty hostess and her situation.

"You certainly have designs upon her, don't you?" inquired Brian.

"Did you have any doubts about it?" asked him Lennart. "If so, then I'm glad to inform you that I'm planning to take her to Aargh with me."

"As your wife?" wanted Brian to know.

"Surely, she can't possibly expect me to marry her," said Lennart, surprised. "Anyway, why the heck do you want to know all this? It's entirely my business."

"Because I feel responsible for the girl," informed him Brian.

"Responsible, you. After what you have done to her —."

"I made her one of the richest women in Aranipor at the age of 23, which is not bad at all," stated Brian. "She is respectable and can pick and choose suitors. You, on the other hand, are planning to make her your mistress, Len."

"Which suitors are you talking about?" asked him Lennart. "You mean locals? She'd be better off as my mistress than married to any of them!"

"Not everybody is so arrogant as you are," said Brian. "You consider her your inferior, because she is a former slave, but I wouldn't mind to marry a girl in her situation."

"So that's it," said Lennart angrily. "You are planning to marry her for her money, no doubt of that. There is but one little obstacle, she doesn't love you. Stay away from her, Brian. This time I'm not going to let her be taken away from me."

"She may love you, but it's hardly a reciprocal feeling," retorted Brian. "Because if you really loved her, you'd marry her, but you don't know what love is. You are simply incapable of normal human feelings."

"And the only love which you know, is love for money," stated Lennart. "Don't try to interfere between us, Brian, if you value your life just a little bit." He stood up, threw a coffee cup which he was holding in his hand on the floor and left.

When staying in D'haki's house Lennart always occupied the same room as on his first visit, and he went there because he wanted to stay alone and to calm down, but upon entering it he ran into Eileen who evidently went there to check if everything was in order. For a moment nobody said anything and then Lennart grabbed her by her arm and looked into her deep blue eyes.

How many times did he dream about them being alone like that, and now his dreams finally came true. For a moment he forgot that the house was full of people, he forgot about Brian and all the rules of decorum and drew her towards himself. She didn't try to resist his embrace, and when he kissed her, her lips were hot and her response passionate.

He tore away the black veil which covered her hair and threw it on the floor, and removed her black cloak; his arm touched her breasts and he felt how she was trembling. Lennart pulled her down and they fell upon the floor together breathing heavily. Lennart could hear his own heart beating fast, and he was coarsely whispering in Aarghean: "Darling, oh darling, I have waited so long."

His hand pulled her skirt up. Suddenly she seemed to come back to her senses. "No," she said, "no, don't do it." Lennart stopped and looked at her stunned. Her cheeks were crimson, and she averted her eyes. "Not here," she whispered, "not now...not in this manner." Lennart slowly realized that she was right and drew back. They both rose to their feet, arranging their clothes, Eileen still avoiding to look at him. She seemed embarassed.

"I'm sorry," apologized Lennart, taking her by her delicate hand. "I didn't mean to, I just...just lost my head." She nodded and looked at him.

"You know that I love you, Captain Duncan," she said quietly, "but we have to wait. The mourning period is not over yet."

It's less than two months now," replied Lennart, "and then we'll go to Aargh together, you and I, Eileen." She looked at him, puzzled.

"You want me to go with you to Aargh, Captain, as your wife?"

"As my...housekeeper," answered Lennart.

She pulled her hand out of his and said sharply: "You mean as your mistress. And your wife will be that Deltan girl? She'll bear you children, and I, what will happen to me when you tire of me, Captain Duncan?"

"Brian told you," said Lennart through his teeth. "I'll wring his neck. Pity I didn't shoot him back on Aargh, when I had a chance, but better late than never."

The expression on his face frightened her and she stood in front of him, barring the way out. "No, don't do it, Captain, don't do it," she repeated, scared. "That won't lead to any good."

"You seem to be genuinely worried about Alistair's well being, don't you?" inquired Lennart. "Coincidentally he spends all his free time in this house with you, trying to convince others that it's purely because of the matters of business, but I'm not such a fool as you both seem to think."

"You are unjust to him, Captain," she pleaded, "you are unjust to both of us," but Lennart didn't listen any more. He pushed her aside and slamming the door behind him, went to search for Brian.

Chapter 2. The Point of No Return

He didn't have to go far as he found Brian in the same place he had left him, in the living-room, drinking another cup of coffee. He seemed quite serene despite their quarel and by some reason it drove Lennart completely mad. Brian heard the door open, turned his head, as he was sitting with his back towards it, and looking into his friend's eyes, saw murder in them.

He jumped to his feet and became rather pale. Brian had known Lennart for many years, and was well aware that under his usual reserve he concealed a temper; and he also had a general idea of what his friend was capable of doing when thoroughly provoked, but he had never seen Lennart in such a fit of rage before.

Lennart didn't waste any time on asking questions, he drew his sword and pointed it towards Brian. "We are going to settle the matter of Eileen once and for all, now," he stated, his voice coarse from suppressed emotion. "Defend yourself."

"You are crazy," retorted Brian. "I'm not going to fight with you. In any case, not in this house."

"Here and now," hissed Lennart through his clenched teeth. "You either draw your sword or I'll kill you as you are." He made several steps towards Brian, the latter moved away so as to have a heavy armchair between them.

"You know I have no chance against you," said Brian, "so it will be murder anyway."

"You can die with weapons in your hand or without, the choice is yours," shouted Lennart and made a swift movement with his sword nearly touching Brian's face. That was enough of a provocation for the latter.

"Bloody bastard," he shouted, drawing his sword and attacking Lennart in his turn.

"Hate to disappoint you," said Lennart with a smile, "but I was born after my parents had been legally married for more than ten years, which I'm afraid can't be said about you."

Brian's face became red and he started furiously striking with his sword, but he was unable to break through Lennart's defence. Lennart knew his own advantage and was playing with his friend as the cat plays with the mouse. They were circling the room, causing considerable damage in the process.

The coffee table was turned upside down, the couch damaged irreparably, they trampled on the fallen cups breaking them into small pieces. Finally Lennart had enough of the game and turning quickly dealt a blow which made Brian's hand go numb and sent his sword flying into the opposite direction. Next second, the polariton blade was at his throat.

"You have one minute to say your last prayers," stated Lennart. Both were panting heavily, Brian looking deathly pale. Blood was dripping from his left arm where Lennart's sword slashed through his jacket, and Lennart had a cut on his face, above his right brow, which he got when Brian, fighting desperately, threw a vase at him. He missed but it hit a wall and broke into a thousand pieces, one of which hurt Lennart, but he didn't feel any pain.

He didn't feel anything at all, except the desire to see Brian dead. They both were so preoccupied that they didn't hear the light steps of a woman who entered the room, but suddenly Lennart felt that somebody hung on his right arm, forcing it down, and as through the mist he heard a female screaming: "No, don't do it! Let him go!"

He recognized the voice immediately and the emotion which he heard in it persuaded him that his was a lost cause. She cared for Brian more than she had ever cared for him. Lennart cursed, and threw his sword to the ground. "You may thank her for saving your life, Brian," he said.

Eileen let his arm go and looked around, then turned to both men, Brian still pale from fear, Lennart pale from fury; and they both thought that they had never seen her so angry before. Her dark blue eyes flashed, and she stamped her little foot.

"You should be ashamed of yourselves, both of you!" she screamed. "Look what you have done! The room's totally ruined, you both wounded. The whole house heard it! What will the people say, what will they think of me now? I offered you hospitality in this house, and that's your gratitude? Oh if only my dear husband were alive....We are fighting in a war, but all you can think about are your personal grudges against each other!"

Lennart thought that she looked very cute while saying all this, and she certainly had a character, but he was still mad at her for rejecting him. He didn't say anything, and neither did Brian. She turned and left. Lennart picked up his sword, switched it off and put it away, and taking a bottle of whisky from the bar left the room after her.

A quarter of an hour later Brian found him sitting on the verandah and the amount of whisky in the bottle had diminished considerably. Brian had his arm bandaged, while Lennart didn't bother to put a plaster on his wound, he decided that disinfecting it with whisky would be enough.

"So you are now taking after your Deltan friend," said Brian gloomily. "May I remind you that anti-fever medication doesn't work in combination with alcohol and that tomorrow a certain Mr Smith expects both of us?"

"Go to Hell," said Lennart as an answer and poured himself another glass.

Brian shrugged his shoulders. "As you wish, but remember that I warned you."

Lennart remembered before the night was over and deeply regretted his getting drunk but it was too late. Brian found him the next morning lying in bed with black circles under his eyes and running a high fever, but still in the same lousy mood as the evening before.

"It's not like I didn't warn you," he said, irritated. "Len, why the heck are you behaving like this? What am I supposed to tell Smith? He will be furious. I'm going to ask Eileen to come and stay with you."

"No, thanks," said Lennart, rising in his bed. "I don't want to see her. Neither do I want to see you. Get out of my room. As for Smith —," but before he could finish his sentence, his last strength left him and he fell back in bed and closed his eyes.

"Bother," muttered Brian, leaving the room. He came back with Eileen, who had red eyes as one who had cried the whole night. Lennart didn't try to protest when they made him take his medicine, in fact he didn't talk at all. He just turned his head away and stared at the wall. The medicine started working and he fell asleep, and when he woke up he saw Brian sitting by his bed. It was getting dark and the lamp was burning.

"You were talking in your sleep," said Brian. "I have never heard you talk before, in whatever state, but this time you did."

"What did I say?" inquired Lennart. By some reason he didn't feel angry any more, at least not towards Brian. They had been through many things together and he realized he didn't want to throw it all away because of a girl. "It's up to her to choose," he thought, "if she chooses Brian, so be it."

"A whole lot in Deltan," replied Brian. "I couldn't understand. Something about your father and somebody called Harry."

"Harry is my eldest brother," said Lennart. "Was it all?"

"You were talking to Miss Nerts. You said something like 'I think you were right, Miss Nerts. You were right.' Who is this Miss Nerts, Len? You never told me about her before. Is she another girlfriend of yours?"

"Miss Nerts is just a nice old lady," replied Lennart.

Brian grinned: "You have no respect even for old age," and they both laughed.

"Listen, Brian, about yesterday," started Lennart. "I probably went too far, I didn't mean it."

"Yesterday I thought that you did," said Brian. "Eileen told me a couple of things and let me tell you, you have a totally wrong notion about —."

"Enough of it," interrupted him Lennart. "Let's not start it all over again. Better tell me what did Smith say?"

"He wished you a speedy recovery," replied Brian, "but he was not amused by you falling ill like that. He expected us to leave tomorrow, but I'm afraid it's impossible. Anyway, he insists that we stay no longer than two extra days on Volcan; it seems we have to hurry because the powers that be have decided that the Great Rebellion should begin in a week. The base on Fern must be evacuated before it starts. There is a lot of work to do, still, and so on and so forth. Well, you know his manner of speaking."

"I'm feeling much better already," stated Lennart. "I think the day after tomorrow will be fine with me."

"I said two extra days," insisted Brian. "Remember, you are our first pilot and I want you to be in top condition. You need your rest. By the way, I much appreciate that you agreed to go to Tarna with me, Len. I didn't expect it."

"You need someone to keep an eye on you," said Lennart.

Two days later, in the early morning, Lennart was packing his things. He was still not feeling at his best, but the orders were clear. They had to leave today. There was a light knock on the door, and Lennart said, "come in." He thought it was a servant bringing him a cup of coffee, but instead he saw Eileen. She went inside and stopped abruptly, as if unsure what to do next.

"Good morning, madam," said Lennart. She looked at him and said suddenly, "Don't go."

Lennart was so surprised that he dropped the official tone he had decided to adopt when speaking to her and asked, "What do you mean, Eileen?"

"Don't go with Alistair, Captain," she repeated. "You won't come back if you do."

"Nonsense," said Lennart. "Besides, I have to; there is no turning back now. I'm afraid we are all past the point of no return." She tried to conceal her tears, but wasn't very successful.

"Why do you care anyway?" inquired Lennart. "After all what happened?"

"You don't understand, Captain," she whispered. "I...I love you. But I can't become your mistress. What would you say if your sister received a proposal like that?"

"I have no sister," said Lennart. "But if I had one....Well, I'd hope that were she to become a slave she'd have a good sense to die."

She looked at him as if he struck her, then turned back and left the room. "What have I done?" thought Lennart. "Eileen," he called, "Eileen," but she disappeared, and he didn't dare to wake the whole house up.

When he and Brian were leaving, she went out with them, and her face looked like that of a marble statue. Lennart wished he could tell her that he didn't mean it like this, but didn't find a chance to do it. He gave her one last glance, but she lowered her eyes and went back into the house. The door closed behind her, and Lennart felt that an invisible wall separated them from each other. He burned the last bridge behind him. There was no going back any more.

Chapter 3. Lyrai Mountains

Contrary to all Lennart's expectations they reached Fern without any problems. All was quiet, but it reminded him of the quietness before the storm. The base was evacuated properly and Lennart personally supervised the destruction of all compromising papers. Officially the Fernian company by the name of "The Eagle" which for nearly two years had been conducting the import of agricultural machinery produced on Volcan, underwent bancruptcy, and its last supplies were sold to its Tarnian partners to pay the debt.

The official owner was also leaving for Tarna, where he planned to join the rebels, together with all the company staff. Lennart had to leave the *Fortune* on Fern and to accompany the last transport to Tarna. During their short journey Brian was thoughtful and not talkative at all, contrary to his habit.

"What the heck is wrong with you?" inquired Lennart finally.

"I think I'm not going back to Volcan," was his friend's answer. "My duty lies with my people, on Tarna. You'll have to return alone, Len."

"I'm not sure it's really a good idea," said Lennart. "You are, after all, my business partner. What if you get killed?"

"You'll inherit my share," informed him Brian. "Then you can go on with the company. Smith and K* will probably let you retire now. As for me, I've got more than enough of this cloak and dagger business. I prefer an open war to espionage."

Lennart decided to drop the matter. He understood how his friend felt and didn't think he should interfere with his decision.

Tarna was a planet basically divided into two unequal parts. A bigger part consisting of several provinces was directly ruled by Uranians, and then there was the Tarnian autonomy, which had self-government and was known by the name of the Free Republic of Tarna. Its capital was Melissa. The Republic was de facto ruled by a small group of aristocrats sympathetic to the independence movement, though they didn't dare to demonstrate it openly.

There were free trade and free persons' movement agreements between the autonomy and Fern, and both states were closely connected. The Free Republic was separated from the occupied territories by Lyrai Mountains, with the border going along the river Adya.

To the south, was the territory under the Uranian rule, to the north the autonomy. The Republic also possessed several islands and was economically better developed than the mainland of Tarna, ruled by the enemy. Uranians basically kept the same administrative divisions which had existed when Tarna was still an independent kingdom, and thus it was divided into six provinces with Istar being the capital. That was also the native city of Brian, and it was situated in the central part of the continent.

The province which bordered the autonomy was called Delor and it had always been harboring separatist ideas, its citizens never fully complying with the occupation. The master plan of Delta was to flood them with weapons and to implicitly promise financial and political support, encouraging them to rebel and demand independence.

The low level guerilla war had been going on forever in those parts, and to entice the leaders to rebel against the occupation authorities was not difficult at all. Lennart didn't know all the details of the operation as his own participation in it was restricted to transporting weapons to the autonomy and ensuring that they got over the border safely. He had a vague idea that Ferrash and Smith suspected that somewhere in the chain there was a weak link and that they were afraid of treason at the last moment, as it had so often happened before.

He knew now that they didn't trust Brian, either, but he wasn't sure why. When he arrived to Melissa, he learned that the previous transport had been intercepted by the Uranian authorities, and all the men accompanying it had been killed; that the borders were guarded twice as thoroughly as before, and that few dared to cross them unauthorized.

Thus the task of ensuring that the last party of weapons reached its destination fell to him, Brian and Fernians. They were with a group of seven men, plus the locals, all together forty people and four trucks. Their plan was to cross the border, split into four groups and deliver the weapons to four different villages.

The Fernians were to stay there, Lennart and Brian who belonged to one group, were supposed to return back to Melissa. The operation was thoroughly thought out; the time was chosen when the mountain area was out of reach of the Uranian satellite. The border was guarded, but there was a four standard hours interval between two patrols and they were supposed to use that time to cross the border and disperse.

The first part of their journey went fine. The enemy didn't expect them, the way was free, and they crossed the border without any problems. The large group split, and Lennart, Brian and eight Tarnians followed the narrow mountain road.

They had to bring the truck to a certain place and to leave it there for the locals to unload by night, and the next day to return to the autonomy. They reached the place when it was getting dark and there they had to wait for several hours till midnight.

Lennart was lying on the grass looking at the stars and thinking how different they were from those on his own planet. Brian sat close to him, cleaning his rifle. Their guide, Wallace, was looking at his watch, worried: the local support group was five minutes late. Suddenly they all heard footsteps, and the guard came back to inform them that he had seen a man walking in the direction of the camp, alone.

Lennart sat up as his instinct which had saved his life so many times before told him that he was in danger. Automatically he disengaged the safety mechanism on his rifle, then looked at Brian and saw him doing the same. They were staying in a narrow valley and the path which led to it from the village was partly covered by a hanging rock.

Wallace, who had left them to meet the approaching person, came back with a smile. "It's OK," he stated, "it's one of the village elders, Anthony; he has been working for us for a long time."

Brian relaxed, but Lennart by some strange reason still had a feeling of coming doom. He stayed aside and kept an eye on Anthony, who was now talking to Wallace. "He says that the men from the village are on the way," informed him Brian who came up and stood by his side.

Anthony smiled, shook hands with Wallace and went back into the darkness, and at that moment Lennart saw a group of men approaching and heard Anthony say, "Here they are".

The enemy opened fire without any warning, and it was only Lennart's quick reaction which saved his life. Brian fell to the ground close to him, and covered by the truck they both kept on shooting. Uranians apparently didn't expect any resistance. There were with a small company and they pulled back.

Lennart saw it as their only chance. Four Tarnians were dead, but four others, including Wallace, stayed alive. Lennart was nearly sure he got Anthony, and that was some comfort to him, though a small one. "Come on," he shouted in Westen, "our only chance is to try and get back."

The men listened to him. With Brian covering them and Lennart leading the way, they were retreating back into the valley, which was wider at the further end of it. The enemy didn't follow them. Lennart estimated that at least half of them were dead or wounded and that probably prevented them from attempting the pursuit.

"Don't count on them letting us go," shouted Brian to Lennart as they were madly climbing a mountain slope. "They'll intercept us on the way back. Right now they are talking on the radio, asking for helicopters."

"Oh, shut up," replied Lennart. He knew they still had about five hours to go, and the way back was probably barred, but he still didn't lose hope.

After they became convinced that there was no pursuit, they stopped and held a council. Wallace was pale and breathing heavily, one of the Tarnians was wounded, he had lost a lot of blood and was close to fainting. They bound up his wound as well as they could, and tried to decide what to do.

"Our only hope is to cross the border," stated Lennart. "Wallace, you know all the mountain paths, where do you think they will least expect us?"

"We can try the Breakaway Pass," said Wallace in an uncertain voice, "but it's a longer distance, and the way there is hard. I'm not sure if Ted will make it," he added, pointing to the wounded man.

"We'll carry him," said Lennart.

It was a very long night and though Ted died a couple of hours later, and they left his body behind, their journey was still physically exhausting. Finally, the skies started turning gray, it was dawn.

"We are nearly there," said Wallace, pointing with his right hand. "Look, we'll cross the river here, and then up that mountain, and we are safe."

Lennart wanted to believe him and nearly convinced himself that they would make it across the border, but at that moment he saw the enemy soldiers. They were coming from the southeast trying to cut off Lennart's small group from the river.

Their last fight was desperate and Lennart knew that if not for him and Brian, the Tarnians wouldn't have the slightest chance. As soldiers, they were no good at all, but he wouldn't give up, and their stubborn resistance threw the enemy back and gave them a chance to escape, but to cross the border they had to go through an open space. Lennart and Brian looked at each other.

"You lead them, Brian," said Lennart. "I'll stay back and cover you."

"I'm not sure," started Brian, but Lennart interrupted him. "Do what I say. That's an order."

"OK," said Brian. They shook hands, and neither said another word.

Lennart decided to give them fifteen minutes and then to try and follow. He was still unscathed, as if by a miracle, and finally he thought that the time had come. He ran half of the distance, turned back to fire at the enemy and at that moment he was hit. His left shoulder felt numb, and there was suddenly mist before his eyes, then everything became dark. Lennart fell to the ground and saw and heard no more.

Chapter 4. An Old Acquaintance

When he came back to his senses he, for a long time, couldn't understand where he was or remember what had happened to him. There was a ringing noise in his ears, and the mist before his eyes prevented Lennart from seeing clearly. He dimly realized that he was lying in bed with a needle stuck into his right arm.

There were men around him talking in a language which sounded vaguely familiar, though Lennart couldn't understand it. The mist became thinner and Lennart saw a figure bend over him and when he could finally focus his eyes properly he came to the conclusion that he had seen the man before, though he couldn't recollect where. "Captain Duncan," said the man, then repeated, "Captain Duncan, can you hear me?"

Lennart recognized the voice and suddenly remembered everything and realized what had happened. He was taken prisoner and the man in front of him was his old acquaintance, Jinescu!

"I see that you recognize me, Captain," said the latter and his voice sounded satisfied. He turned to the other man present who was wearing a medical uniform and started talking in Uranian. Lennart closed his eyes. He deeply regretted that he had stayed alive. It could end but in one manner for him anyway, and he didn't look forward to being interrogated by Jinescu.

He must have lost his consciousness again, and when he finally woke up he was alone in what looked like a hospital room, dressed in pajamas, covered with bandages, but the needle was gone. The door opened and a middle-aged man with a pleasant face came in, who judging by his clothes was a doctor. He had dark eyes and dark hair and looked apprehensive.

"Good morning," he said in Westen, speaking with a slight accent. "I'm Doctor Frances. How do you feel, Captain?"

"Lousy," said Lennart. "I guess I should thank you for saving my life, although I wish you hadn't done it."

"Do you think you are able to answer questions?" asked Frances, ignoring Lennart's impolite tone.

"Does it matter whether I say 'yes' or 'no'?" inquired Lennart.

"Colonel Jinescu insists on talking to you," said Frances apologizingly. At that moment the door opened and Jinescu came in and sat on a chair by the bed.

"I see you are much better today, Captain Duncan," he observed.

"Congratulations on your promotion," said Lennart.

"Thank you," replied Jinescu. "I happen to be in charge on this military base, Captain Duncan, and you can't imagine how thrilled I was to discover that the man who had been taken prisoner, was you. I still remember our previous conversation and can't wait until you tell me more about this perfectly legal business of yours."

Lennart turned away and stared at the wall in front of him.

"Do you have nothing to say?" insisted Jinescu. "Last time you were more talkative."

"I suffer from amnesia," said Lennart. "As a result of a concussion. Can't remember anything at the moment."

"Well, I'll be happy to remind you the circumstances which led to your capture, Captain," told him Jinescu apparently enjoying the situation. "You were captured with weapons in your hands while fighting the lawful authorities. I hope you understand the implications of this. Your only chance to save your life is to answer my questions truthfully. Now what were you doing in the mountains?"

"Which mountains?" asked Lennart.

"Lyrai mountains," said Jinescu. "You'd better think of a credible story, Captain, otherwise your future will look very grim."

"Well," started Lennart, "I went on vacation to Tarna and decided to camp in the mountains, with a guide and a couple of locals, we lost our way and then we were suddenly attacked by a group of armed men. While defending myself I got wounded, the rest I don't remember."

"I expected something better than this," remarked Jinescu. "Do you seriously think I'll believe you?" Lennart didn't reply.

"Enough," interrupted Frances. "He lost a lot of blood and needs rest. You can interrogate him tomorrow, when he is feeling better."

Jinescu rose up, went to the side table and took a sheet of paper lying over there. He scanned it and then turned to the doctor.

"You are giving him morphine," he said.

"Otherwise he won't be able to sleep," declared Frances.

"I suggest that you stop doing it. It may help Captain Duncan refresh his memory."

Frances apparently didn't agree and they started arguing in Uranian. Lennart had the feeling that Jinescu got the last word. He left the room and Frances muttered something incomprehensible. The next several hours seemed very long to Lennart. The impact of the last injection was wearing off and he was feeling progressively worse. His left arm was already severely damaged and the recent wound didn't improve the situation.

In the evening the pain became unbearable, he was unable to eat and just lay staring at the ceiling and biting on his lips in order not to groan. He was largely left alone during the day, but in the evening Frances came in to check on him. He looked at Lennart's face, said something which sounded like a curse, left and then came back with a syringe in his hand.

"You'll get into trouble because of it," said Lennart watching Frances roll up his sleeve.

"I don't care," said Frances.

"It's awfully decent of you, Doctor," stated Lennart. "I'm sorry about this morning."

"Never mind," replied Frances. "Just try to get some sleep before tomorrow."

The next day Lennart felt much better even though he was still unable to use his left arm. He got quite a good breakfast, but after washing himself in an adjacent small bathroom he went back to bed. Lennart considered it was in his immediate interest to pretend that he was sicker than he really felt.

Jinescu didn't make him wait long; he appeared soon afterwards, looked at his prisoner's face and inquired, "Still can't remember anything, Captain?"

"No, not much," replied Lennart. Jinescu smiled, showing his white teeth. "Let's start from the very beginning, Captain. What were you doing in the Lyrai Mountains?"

The conversation between them went in circles, and after an hour or so they both seemed to get rather tired of each other. Jinescu left and Lennart, who got a headache, fell asleep, but after a couple of hours Jinescu came back and on and on it went. He knew a lot already and basically demanded from Lennart to reveal the whole scheme, being especially interested in the role of the Deltan government in it.

After several hours of a very one-sided conversation Lennart, who got pain in his shoulder again, felt as if he was going mad. Jinescu finally decided to leave, and Lennart got another night of sleep only due to Frances's kindness. It went on for three consecutive days by the end of which Lennart got the feeling that he and Jinescu were becoming thoroughly sick of each other. On the fourth day Jinescu entered the room with a triumphant expression on his face.

"I have a surprise for you, Captain," he said, and made a sign to one of the guards who usually accompanied him. The man went out and returned with two other soldiers and a handcuffed prisoner in whom Lennart recognized Brian. He rose from his bed and stared at him in astonishment.

"What are you doing here?" he inquired in Aarghean.

"I'd ask you to use the language we all can understand," said Jinescu, who was thoroughly enjoying the scene. "We arrested this friend of yours yesterday evening. It was rather unwise of him to hang so close to the border after what had happened, but he was apparently wondering about your fate, Captain. A very touching example of true friendship." Brian's face expression persuaded Lennart that the colonel was speaking the truth. Jinescu continued.

"That young man made a statement this morning which basically confirmed my suspicions that both of you were in the service of Delta." Lennart looked at Brian inquiringly and his friend averted his eyes.

"It's no use denying the obvious," he said in a low voice, speaking Westen. "They know too much already. That's our only chance, Len."

"What will you say to it, Captain?" inquired Jinescu.

"Name: Lennart Duncan. Rank: captain. Personal number: 9910789ABD, and that's all the information I'm required to give," said Lennart

"That's at least something," remarked Jinescu with a peculiar look in his eyes. "99 is a code for the military intelligence of Delta, isn't it, Captain? Strange that your friend got the number wrong." He looked at Brian closely and then continued. "I guess it's because you are one of those independent contractors Deltans are known to be widely using nowadays, aren't you?"

Brian said nothing and neither did Lennart. There was a pause, and Jinescu was the first who spoke: "There is a proverb which states that one who says 'A' should say 'B' as well. I need the information you can provide and I'm determined to get it. You both may choose to cooperate of your own free will and save us all a lot of trouble. You have one hour to decide."

Brian was escorted out of the room and Jinescu left after him. He went into his office and Major Lukan, an officer who had assisted him during the interrogations followed him together with Frances.

"I need to talk to you, Colonel," said Lukan decisively. "We can't torture the prisoners. It's against the convention."

"And Duncan is wounded as well," added Frances.

"The convention doesn't protect terrorists and enemy agents," remarked Jinescu.

"Captain Duncan is an officer in the army of Delta," insisted Lukan. "He falls into the category of a prisoner of war."

"Does he?" inquired Jinescu. "Last time I checked we are not at war with Delta, and Duncan wasn't captured wearing a uniform. The discussion is closed, gentlemen, but to ease your conscience, we'll start with the other. And we are not going to torture him, either, just to use enhanced interrogation techniques."

An hour later Lennart wearing his old torn clothes and handcuffed despite the doctor's protests was standing in the interrogation room and watching the preparations for Brian to be waterboarded. They both had to undergo it as a part of their officer training on Aargh, but Lennart wasn't sure Brian would be able to withstand it. In fact, he wasn't sure he was able to do it, either.

"You can save him the ordeal, Captain," stated Jinescu. "If you wish to. Just give us a sign and we'll stop."

Lennart had to stand still and watch and if he tried to turn away or simply change his position a guard would hit him. He soon lost all the notion of time, but on the outside he managed to look composed, which in fact, as he was well aware, irritated the colonel profoundly. He also had an idea that Brian would have spoken long ago, were it not for his presence.

It went on for more than two hours but ended rather abruptly. Lennart had a feeling that a couple of his ribs were broken and had to fight against a spell of dizziness. He turned away and at that moment the guard hit him hard across his chest, the rifle butt slipped and came with full force upon Lennart's bad shoulder. Lennart saw stars and fainted.

When he came back to his senses he was sitting on a chair in Jinescu's office, with Lukan at his side. "Are you feeling better, Captain?" asked the latter. Lennart didn't reply. He didn't feel like talking at all. His wound started bleeding again and his clothes were drenched with fresh blood. Jinescu went in and gave an order in Uranian. Lukan evidently objected, but to no avail.

Lennart was put back on his feet by two guards and they dragged him out, then along the narrow corridor and into another room, with a metal rack in it. Lennart realized what it meant only too well, but didn't try to resist when they stripped him of his shirt and chained him up. The voltage was being increased slowly and the pain was excruciating, so that Jinescu finally got the result he wanted: to see his prisoner lose his cold reserve, scream and convulse, trying in vain to break his chains; but the only thing he got out of him were curses in three languages.

Lennart was covered with blood from his wound and he was losing the last strength. He thought that Jinescu ordered to increase the voltage and hoped that he would get a heart attack and die. He made the last desperate attempt to free himself, saw a flash of light in front of his eyes and then everything went black, and when he opened his eyes again, he was lying in the same hospital bed with Frances standing above him and swearing in Uranian.

Chapter 5. Brian

For the rest of that day Lennart was left alone, and he didn't see anyone except the doctor who gave him another morphine shot so that he could sleep through the night. The next morning, soon after breakfast, the door opened and Jinescu came in. He was accompanied by two soldiers as usual, and they stayed by the door, while he sat on the chair by Lennart's bed. "Good morning, Captain," he said.

Lennart had such profound hatred for the man that he didn't feel capable of answering politely, so he just turned his head away. It didn't discourage the colonel in the slightest. He opened a file he had in his hands, took a laminated sheet of paper out of it and started reading.

When Lennart heard the first words he turned his head and stared at Jinescu. The paper in question contained the full confession which included names, dates and in short, all the details of the operation. Lennart listened attentively, not being able to take his eyes off the colonel's face. The confession was several pages long and was signed "Benjamin Amman." Jinescu finished reading and looked at Lennart, who was sitting in bed by now.

"Well, Captain Duncan, what will you say to this?"

"What did you do to him?" asked Lennart in a coarse voice. "Sticking needles under his nails?"

Jinescu smiled. "There was no need to do it. We just showed him a video made during your interrogation of yesterday afternoon. This in combination with a couple of showers your friend had to undergo yesterday morning convinced him to cooperate."

He paused waiting for Lennart to say something, but the latter was unable to speak so Jinescu continued.

"I figured out that one of you would talk, and I came to the conclusion that you, Captain, were inclined to become a martyr for the cause; which, in my opinion, could not be said about that friend of yours, and I was right. You see, the difference between the two of you is that you'd rather die, but Amman would rather stay alive."

Lennart fell back in bed. He felt empty inside. Jinescu won and they both knew it. The colonel was apparently savoring the situation.

"You should have never come to Tarna, Captain. It's a lost cause, it will never be free. Now that you have seen Tarnians in action it must be obvious to you that the rebellion is doomed. They will never win against us."

"They lack experience," said Lennart, "but they will learn."

"It's not the combat skills that they lack," retorted Jinescu. "What they lack is warrior spirit. You see, Captain, all men in the world could be divided into masters and slaves. Tarnians are a slave race."

"And you surely think that you belong to the master race?" asked Lennart indignantly.

"As do you," replied the colonel. "Deltans are a formidable enemy, and I will be the first to admit it. However, you have no business on Tarna."

"I usually leave politics to my superiors," said Lennart, "otherwise I could tell you, Colonel, that Tarna used to be very much our business, and we have just as much right to be there as you."

Jinescu shrugged his shoulders. "It was more than seventy years ago, Captain, which is a very long time. Anyway, this conversation is pointless. I give you five minutes to get dressed and then I'll meet you in my office." He stood up and left.

Ten minutes later Lennart, handcuffed and escorted by four soldiers, was brought to Jinescu's office. The first person he saw when he came in was his friend, also handcuffed; four more soldiers and a young lieutenant whose name he wasn't sure of.

"Hello, Brian," said Lennart, calling his friend by his Aarghean name. Brian didn't answer; he avoided looking at Lennart at all. At that moment, the door opened again and Lucan came in, with a notebook in his hands. He started talking to Jinescu in a low voice while showing him something on the computer screen. Jinescu looked satisfied; he nodded and then addressed Brian in Westen, so that Lennart would be able to understand him, too.

"You told us that you had Volcanian nationality, mister Amman, didn't you? And that your Christian name was Benjamin. This gentleman calls you Brian, which he undoubtedly has a good reason for; but once you had a third name as well, or should I say the first one?"

Brian became suddenly very pale, but kept silence and Jinescu continued his story. "The name given you at birth was Edward Vine, wasn't it? You very conveniently forgot to mention it while giving your testimony."

Brian looked up. "You promised me life," he said speaking with difficulty. "You said you'd let me go."

“Sure,” agreed Jinescu, “but it was before I knew your true identity, Mr Vine. Now when I found out that you had been sentenced to death in absentia by the military court of Istar in the year ’16, there is nothing left for me to do but to carry out the sentence.”

“You lied to me,” screamed Brian. “You knew from the very beginning that I was born on Tarna! You gave me your word and now you are breaking it.”

“I don’t think you have a reason to complain,” remarked Jinescu who stayed unmoved, “after all we aren’t going to hang you. I took into consideration the fact that you provided us with valuable information which it would have otherwise probably taken us weeks to get out of Captain Duncan.” He turned to Lukan and started speaking in Uranian.

Brian seemed to compose himself. “I have a last wish,” he said. “I want to talk to him,” and he pointed to Lennart, “in private. Give me five minutes.”

Jinescu seemed to hesitate. “I’m not sure it’s a good idea, to allow you two to communicate secretly,” he said finally, “but under these circumstances...well, you have your five minutes.”

Lennart and Brian were left alone, with guards standing in a semi-circle around them, but keeping some distance.

“So you hoped they’d execute me and let you go, didn’t you?” inquired Lennart. “Then you’d probably state that I was a traitor and, of course, I’d be dead and not able to defend myself. Pity it didn’t work like that.”

“Shut up and listen,” said Brian. “It’s about Eileen. I think I should let you know just what an idiot you have been all the time. You could have been very happy together if not for your arrogance. Eileen was never a prostitute. She was to be sold as a virgin, because virgins bring much more money, and the only man in her life was D’haki, her husband, who bought her with the intention to marry her.”

“Why did you never tell me this before?” inquired Lennart, stunned.

“Because you never asked,” replied Brian.

“Then why are you telling me all this now?”

“After D’haki’s death I wanted to marry her,” said Brian, “but she chose you, and you treated her abominably. Since I’m sure that you’ll follow me soon enough, I want your last dying thought be one of remorse and realization of the fact that you won’t be able to set it right. Consider it my revenge.”

He turned and said something in Uranian, addressing Jinescu and the latter nodded, pointed to Lennart and said to Lukan: "Take this one out as well and place him where he can see everything."

It was chilly outside, and the sky was covered with gray clouds. Lennart felt cold and strangely numb. He looked at his friend, blindfolded, standing in front of the firing squad and suddenly said in Aarghean: "I forgive you, Brian. Die in peace."

It all seemed unreal to him, like in a bad dream when one tries to wake up and can't. He saw the soldiers fire and his friend's body hit the ground, saw Lukan checking the pulse, then talking to Jinescu, apparently asking what to do with him, but outwardly he kept calm. He just watched with an immovable face. Time seemed to stand still.

"What about Captain Duncan?" asked Lukan meanwhile.

"Take him away and lock him up in a cell," ordered Jinescu. "We'll decide what to do with him later."

Lennart fully expected to be the next victim and was very much surprised when instead they took him back into the building and locked him up in a basement which was used as a prison. His cell had one small window, barred, through which he could see exactly the part of the inner yard where Brian had died; and its furniture consisted of a dirty mattress lying on the cement floor and a sanitary installation behind a thin partition wall. The only source of light besides the window was a dim lamp in the ceiling.

When the heavy door closed, Lennart sank on the mattress. Now that he was left alone, his reserve broke and he covered his face with his hands and wept for Brian. It seemed to Lennart that a part of him had died together with his friend and he suddenly felt years older. After some time, he composed himself and started thinking of what Brian had told him, and with a shock remembered his last conversation with Eileen.

How could he have treated her in this manner? How could he be so cruel? Lennart desperately wished he could meet her again to try and apologize, and the impossibility of it drove him mad. His misery reached its highest point when he thought that she could have taken his words seriously and killed herself. Then her death would be upon his conscience. And it might be very soon that he would have to give a report of his deeds to the Heavenly Judge. What would he say?

Lennart started praying fervently, asking God to give him one last chance, one opportunity to set things right. "And if I should die," he added, "let her find a good man and be happy. Let her forget me."

He felt somewhat better after this, and started wondering what Jinescu was planning to do with him. He didn't have to wonder long as the door soon opened again and he saw a lieutenant and a group of soldiers. "Captain Duncan," said the lieutenant, "you have to follow me."

Chapter 6. A Hostage

He was taken through a long narrow corridor and brought into a room which looked like a conference hall, with rows of chairs and a platform with a big table on it. Three men sat behind the table: Jinescu, Lukan and another officer in the rank of captain and Jinescu's secretary, Lieutenant Barrow was sitting at the side of the table. They all looked unusually sober and Lennart realized that he had to undergo some kind of a trial.

"I have forgotten that Uranians are extremely fond of formalities," he thought. "They cannot shoot me without convicting me first."

He guessed correctly, but if he had expected to undergo tiresome interrogations once again he was disappointed, as the whole trial took approximately ten minutes. He had to stand up and listen to his death sentence read by the secretary. Lennart found out that he had been accused, tried and found guilty of espionage, terrorism, smuggling of weapons, taking part in armed insurrection and resisting arrest by the lawful authorities.

On all charges the punishment was death and thus Lennart was sentenced to execution by firing squad. The sentence was signed by Colonel Jinescu, Major Lukan and Captain Marin. Barrow finished reading and there was a pause, then Jinescu asked: "Do you have anything to say, Captain Duncan?"

"I object to the last point," answered Lennart. "How could I have resisted arrest if I was unconscious when your men dragged me away?"

The secretary turned away hastily to conceal a smile.

"You didn't surrender when given a chance," explained Jinescu.

Lennart wanted to say that he had never been given such a chance, but decided it was below his dignity to argue. He shrugged his shoulders and replied: "You decided everything beforehand anyway."

"You didn't expect a trial by jury, did you, Captain?" inquired Jinescu. "Do you have anything else to say? Do you admit your guilt?"

"Whatever I may have done," stated Lennart, "was done in the service of my country or so I thought at the moment. You can be sure that I feel no remorse," he added and looked at Jinescu with a challenge, but to his surprise the latter smiled.

"We have come to the same conclusion, Captain Duncan, and decided to give you one last chance and to make your death sentence conditional."

Lennart was extremely surprised but before he could ask any questions, Jinescu continued: "if your government agrees to fullfill our demands, you will be deported, but once you set foot on any territory controlled by Uranians again you will forfeit your pardon. Deltan authorities will be informed about your fate today and given exactly two weeks to decide whether they accept our conditions. If they refuse or don't respond in time, you'll die. So now your life depends on your own people, Captain."

Lennart tried his best to stay indifferent but he couldn't help asking, "What are these conditions, Colonel?"

"You've probably heard about the election of the governor to be held in Aranipor the next month?" inquired Jinescu. "Your government supports one of the candidates and he has a very good chance of winning. Our demand is that your government steps back and lets the election take its course without any political pressure from their side."

"So you decided to use me as a hostage," said Lennart bitterly. "We both know they will never agree to these conditions, so the delay has no sense."

"Are you so eager to die, Captain?" asked Jinescu. "In my opinion, we are giving you a fair chance, considering all your crimes. Delta always states that they value human life highly, so now they will have an opportunity to prove it."

He stood up showing that the discussion was over. Lennart was brought back to his cell where he had ample time to think of what had happened and to estimate his chances. His common sense told him that there was no hope for him whatsoever, but despite this he still hoped that Delta would agree, and this uncertainty was the worst torment one could imagine.

By some reason Lennart was sure that it was exactly what Jinescu was trying to achieve, to break him down completely. The cell was cold at night and he wasn't even given a blanket, he didn't have any medical attendance, the chains which he had to wear were heavy and forced his left arm into a very uncomfortable position, and after a couple of days he caught cold and started coughing heavily. Finally on the fourth day a guard found him lying unconscious and informed Lukan, who in his turn, after talking to Frances went to see Jinescu together with him.

"It can't go on like this, sir," said Lukan. "The prisoner needs urgent medical attention, otherwise the doctor here tells me he will die."

"Yes, it's true," supported him Frances. "He's probably developed pneumonia, and will surely die if left to himself. Though it's probably exactly what you wish, Colonel."

"You are mistaken, gentlemen. I don't want Captain Duncan to die before his time," said Jinescu.

"Then you don't object to him being transferred back to the hospital, sir?" inquired Lukan.

"On your own responsibility, Major. If he escapes —."

"He is in no state to escape anywhere," interrupted the doctor. I'll give you my word for this, Colonel."

"Very well," said Jinescu. "Do what you consider necessary to save his life."

Thus Lennart came back to his senses once again in the same hospital bed with a needle sticking in his arm and the first person he encountered was Frances.

"Saving me for the gallows, Doctor?" he inquired rather rudely. "Why can't you let me die on my own?"

"I'm just doing my duty," replied Frances. "You shouldn't talk of dying, Captain. I'm sure you will be exchanged."

"And I'm sure I won't be," said Lennart gloomily and started coughing.

He did get a heavy case of pneumonia on top of other things and spent the next four days in bed, but gradually recovered and was put back to prison, but this time without handcuffs, and with warm blankets, and Frances and Lukan coming every day to check on him. He was even taken outside for a walk and in general treated more or less well.

Lukan seemed to feel sincere sympathy towards Lennart and would just drop by to find out if he needed anything. Lennart considered it best to keep a distance, which he did in a polite and formal manner. He came to the conclusion that among Uranians there were decent people, too, and that he couldn't judge them all by Colonel Jinescu. Time went on, and with each day Lennart's hope diminished, and finally fourteen days were over.

Lukan had to come to Jinescu's office and he didn't exactly feel like it. The colonel was sitting at his table with a cup of coffee in his hand and a coffee pot standing in front of him. He offered a cup to his officer, but Lukan, who looked rather pale, refused.

"Still no answer from Delta, sir?" he asked, and Jinescu shook his head.

"No, I'm afraid not. You understand what it means so I want you to go to Duncan and inform him that he is to die tomorrow."

"Why can't we just deport him, sir?" inquired Lukan.

"Because he is a convicted criminal?" asked Jinescu. "Or may be because he is one of those responsible for the recent outbreak of the civil war, which thank Heaven, is drawing to its end? Yes, probably that's why. Actually, I find it strange, Major, that you take such an interest in the fate of an enemy agent."

"Captain Duncan is just an officer who was serving his country," insisted Lukan. "Anyone of us could be in his place."

"But we are not," said Jinescu. "And his own side doesn't seem to care much about what happens to him, so why should we? May I remind you, Major, that you also signed his death sentence?"

"When I did it, I thought he would be exchanged," replied Lukan hopelessly. "Also, if Duncan is to die, isn't it cruel to make him wait till tomorrow morning, after he had to wait for two weeks to know his fate?"

"You see it all wrong, Major," stated Jinescu. "I just want to give Captain Duncan some extra time, one last chance, so to say. Now enough said. Go to him and ask if he needs anything. Seeing a priest or something."

"You forget, sir, that Duncan belongs to a different church," remarked Lukan. "I don't think he'll want our priest."

"Then may be he'll want something else," said Jinescu impatiently. "Writing a letter to his family, or something to the point. He may do it if he wishes so. Don't hang around here, Major, and keep in mind that tomorrow I expect you to be present as well."

Lukan said, "yes, sir", and left abruptly. He found his prisoner sitting on the mattress with his back to the wall, wrapped in a blanket, reading an old car magazine which Lukan had lent him. He seemed to be rather absorbed in it, but raised his head to greet the major.

Lukan suddenly had difficulty speaking, but finally he forced himself to do it.

"I regret to tell you, Captain, but we still...there has still been no answer from Delta. Do you realize what it means?"

"Yes, I do," said Lennart slowly. "When am I to die?"

"Tomorrow morning at six," replied Lukan. "Do you need anything? Writing a letter to your family, for instance?"

"They will be no doubt informed," said Lennart dryly. "You can send them a video, though."

"It's forbidden to film executions," stated Lukan. "You aren't married, Captain, are you?"

"No, thank God," answered Lennart. "There will be no widow and orphans left to fend for themselves." He suddenly fell silent. When Lukan mentioned his family he thought of his father first, but now he remembered someone else.

"You know, Major, I do want to write a letter after all," he said. "If you give me your word that the person in question will get it. It's a lady, you see."

"I give you my word of honor," assured him Lukan solemnly. "Tonight at 9 p.m. a mail ship is leaving and your letter will go with it. I'll see to it personally, Captain."

"That's awfully nice of you," said Lennart.

He was provided with some paper, a pen and an envelope and left alone, but writing this letter proved a much more difficult task than Lennart had ever expected it to be. He had to tear up several copies until finally he was more or less satisfied with the result. That's what his letter said:

Dear Eileen,

This will be my last letter to you, and I'm writing it from a Uranian military prison on Tarna. Brian is dead, and now my turn has come to follow him. Before I die, I want to apologize for my cruel words to you, which I now know, were based on a false assumption. I only hope that you will be able to forgive me, and I want you to know that I have never loved any other woman but you. Please try to forget me, as you are too young to spend your life mourning, when you could make some man very happy.

Yours truly,

Lennart

He closed the envelope, wrote the address upon it, and handed the letter over to Lukan. The door was closed and he was left alone. Lennart suddenly remembered the words out of the oath of allegiance to the Kingdom of Delta: "...I swear by my honor to fight and to die, if necessary, cheerfully; knowing that no destiny is better than to give one's life for his Fatherland; so help me God."

"I wonder what did they mean by dying cheerfully?" he thought. By some strange reason Lennart didn't feel particularly cheerful and he could think of a much better destiny than the one which awaited him the next morning. He was only twenty eight and not yet tired of his life. He finally realized that till the very last moment he still had hope, but now it was all over for him.

Lennart looked back upon his whole life and asked himself probably for the first time if he had done everything right. He had always been a self-assured person, not really prone to any doubt, until now. He knew he was far from being a saint, but despite this he had always tried to act according to his ideas of honor and duty. He then thought of his father. "Well, here's one positive thing in this whole story," he said to himself. "Since tomorrow, the issue of my mother won't be between him and me any more, it will be between him and God."

It was getting late, and outside it was dark. Lennart said a prayer for the remission of his sins and for an easy death and sank upon his mattress. Contrary to his own expectations, he soon fell asleep.

Chapter 7. Miss Nerts Gives Advice

Miss Nerts sat alone in her living-room, knitting. It was after 10 p.m. and her housekeeper, who kept early hours, was already in bed. The maid had asked for an extra free evening, she was going to get married soon and Miss Nerts thought with regret about losing her. It had been rather difficult to find good servants lately, but the maid was a sweet country girl and Miss Nerts wished her all the happiness in the world.

The house was quiet as the TV set was off. One could hear the old cuckoo clock ticking. Suddenly the door bell rang. Miss Nerts looked surprised. Sarah, the maid, would use a reserve key and it was rather late for visitors. She stood up and went to the door.

"Who is there?" asked Miss Nerts rather uncertainly, and to her amazement she heard the answer, "Cousin George."

She opened the door and Colonel Ferrash came in. "Well, I never," said Miss Nerts rather discomposed. "What on Earth brings you here at this hour?" Ferrash didn't answer but sank into a chair with a distressed expression on his face. Miss Nerts opened the bar and took a whisky bottle out of it. She poured some whisky into a glass.

"Enough," said Ferrash. "I have to drive back to North Star in an hour." He took the glass from her hands and drank it all up, then placed the empty glass on the salon table.

"What do you have on your mind, George?" inquired Miss Nerts, after having waited in vain for the colonel to speak.

"I came to ask you to do me a favor," said Ferrash finally. "But now I think I need your advice as well."

"If I can be of any service —." started Miss Nerts, but Ferrash interrupted her.

"It concerns someone you know, though may be not by his real name."

"If you mean Lord Alex, he told me his story," assured him Miss Nerts. "Does he have problems?"

"You seem to know all sorts of things, Miss Nerts," smiled Ferrash faintly. "As for Captain Duncan having problems, well I guess one can say so."

"What sort of problems?" asked Miss Nerts.

"The worst sort possible," said Ferrash gloomily. "He was taken prisoner and they are going to execute him."

"Oh," gasped Miss Nerts, horrified. "Is there nothing you can do to help him?"

"I feel myself responsible for the whole situation," continued Ferrash without taking notice of her question. "I offered him that job. He wanted nothing to do with it and I practically forced him to accept, playing upon his patriotism and sense of duty. I sent him to his death."

"You shouldn't blame yourself, George," said Miss Nerts sympathetically. "You couldn't have known it would turn out like this. But what is it you want me to do?"

"I thought there was a girl involved," answered Ferrash. "His friend's sister. Margaret, I believe, is her name. I wanted to ask you to inform her about Lord Alex's fate. Weren't they engaged or something?"

"Your information is not entirely correct," said Miss Nerts. "Margaret does love Captain Duncan, but he told me he was in love with another woman and that he had informed Margaret about it before leaving. Of course, I will talk to her though I'm afraid it will be a heavy blow for the poor girl. What exactly should I say?"

"Well," began Ferrash, "there is still some hope left that Lord Alex will be....I'm afraid," he interrupted himself, "that I'm not telling this whole story to you in logical order. You see, the enemy offered to exchange him if we fulfill some of their conditions."

"That's good news, then!" exclaimed Miss Nerts. "It would be too bad otherwise."

"That's exactly what I wanted to know your opinion about, Miss Nerts," said Colonel Ferrash. "As you know, some time ago the government fell and the opposition came to power. The new minister of the foreign affairs Lord Henry Nigel has taken a hard line in dealing with...with certain things. In short, the demands of the other side are of a political nature and he adamantly refused to even listen to them. In his opinion, it means to demonstrate our weakness internationally."

"Goodness gracious," exclaimed Miss Nerts. "But, of course, he doesn't know —."

"That it's the life of his own son we are talking about," finished Ferrash.

"Why didn't you tell him?" inquired Miss Nerts.

"Because I promised to Lord Alex that as long as he is alive his father won't learn about the true identity of Captain Duncan. So now I'm not sure what to do, and I wanted to have your advice on the matter."

"I think you should tell him immediately," said Miss Nerts. "He is bound to know later on and he will never forgive himself; and anyway let Lord Henry take an informed decision."

"You really think I ought to break my word?" inquired Ferrash, still not fully convinced.

"I'm perfectly sure," replied Miss Nerts.

"Then I'm going there now," said Ferrash, rising up. "We still have one more day."

"You'll let me know how it will end, won't you?" asked Miss Nerts opening the door.

"I will, and in the meanwhile please pray for him. I'm sure that at the moment Lord Alex needs our prayers."

They parted and Colonel Ferrash drove back to the capital. It was nearly midnight when he finally parked his car in front of the Foreign Affairs Ministry. Lord Henry Nigel was known for keeping late hours and Ferrash hoped he would still find him there and he was not mistaken.

Lord Henry didn't appear especially glad to see him. They had known each other for years though one couldn't say that they were close friends. The 22nd Marquess of Wallistan turned sixty five this year and though his hair was gray, one could still call him a handsome man. He sat at a table covered with papers, and turned away from the computer screen to greet his visitor.

"Please be seated, Colonel. What is this urgent business which brings you here at this hour?"

"It's about an officer of mine, Your Excellency, Captain Duncan," explained Ferrash.

"Yes, I have heard this story," said Lord Henry not much trying to conceal his irritation. "I'm very sorry, Colonel, but I'm afraid there is nothing we can do for him."

"But Your Excellency," protested Ferrash, "the demands of Uranians aren't too unreasonable. The only thing they want from us is that we make an official statement that we endorse neither candidate. Even if it influences the elections in Aranipor, it won't change the situation there much. The governor is just a figurehead, and the power will remain in the hands of the family loyal to our interests. While, on the other hand, we will save a young man's life."

"It's not about the election," explained the minister. "It's about losing face. We can't afford to let Uranians dictate our actions; don't you see it,

Colonel? If we give them a finger this time, next time they will want to have the whole hand. As for that young man, as I have said, I'm sorry, but he is a soldier after all, isn't he? He knew he was risking his life when he took this job. Next time we catch a Uranian agent we'll execute him in retaliation. I hope that will satisfy you."

Ferrash looked at Lord Henry trying to understand whether the latter was speaking seriously. The light blue eyes of the minister had a very familiar expression in them, that of a person who had taken his decision and wasn't going to change it. His Excellency apparently waited for his visitor to leave. Instead, Ferrash took something out of his pocket.

"Before I go, Your Excellency, I would like you to see this," he said. "May be it will make you change your mind on the issue."

He put a small photograph on the table. Lord Henry looked at it and suddenly changed color. He turned to his visitor and asked in a coarse voice: "Whose picture is it, Colonel?"

"Don't you recognize him?" inquired Ferrash. "That's the officer in question, Captain Lennart Duncan, also known as Lord Alex Nigel, your third son."

There was a long pause during which the minister kept staring at the picture, but finally his face took its usual cold expression.

"So that's it, then," he said. "Can you tell me, Ferrash, why should I go against my principles to save his life? After all, this son of mine hasn't been much of a son to me during the last ten years."

"Because you will never forgive yourself, Lord Henry, if you don't," answered Ferrash and added: "And because twelve years ago he went against his principles when he gave a false testimony in court to save you."

"I was not guilty of the crime I had been accused of," stated the minister calmly.

"I know. I conducted a small investigation of my own. But that son of yours didn't."

"You seem to know a lot of things, Colonel," remarked Lord Henry coldly.

"It's my job," replied Ferrash. "So what is your decision, Your Excellency?"

"I need time to think," said the minister.

"But Lord Wallistan, we don't have much time —." started Ferrash, but Lord Henry interrupted him.

"I said that I needed some time to think, Colonel. I have your mobile number and I will contact you when I have taken my decision."

He spoke in a manner of one accustomed to be obeyed and Ferrash understood that the conversation was over. He stood up and said: "Very well, my lord. But while you are thinking this business over, I would ask you to take into consideration the fact that your son underwent torture, that he is wounded and probably denied the necessary medical treatment, and that at this very moment he is awaiting execution in Uranian prison. May be this information will help you to take the correct decision."

He went out and closed the door behind him, leaving Lord Henry deep in thought.

Chapter 8. Lennart Meets His Fate

The next morning Lukan found his prisoner on his feet and awaiting him when the door of his cell opened. Lennart didn't look any different from his usual self, only slightly more serious. He nodded and said, "Good morning, Major," in his usual calm manner, but it cost Lukan some difficulty to answer him in a steady voice.

They went out into the prison yard, Lukan first and Lennart escorted by two guards behind him. Jinescu and Frances were already waiting for them, together with a group of six soldiers. The doctor looked as a person who hadn't slept well, while Jinescu had his usual sarcastic face expression.

The morning air was very cold, and sharp wind was making it even chillier. Lennart had his old torn clothes on, which provided little protection against the wind, and he started coughing heavily. Frances turned his head away, but said nothing. Lennart finally recovered his breath, looked at Jinescu and decided to wish him a good morning as well. He didn't know why but he was sure it would irritate his enemy and he was right. The colonel only nodded impatiently.

They brought Lennart to the wall and then he had to turn and face the firing squad. "Do you have any last wishes, Captain?" asked Jinescu. "A cigaret?"

"I want to die with my eyes open," answered Lennart.

"So be it," said Jinescu.

Just as the soldiers were taking aim, Lennart gathered the remnants of his self-control, looked right in front of himself, raised his chin and smiled his most arrogant smile. At that moment Jinescu's mobile started ringing. The colonel seemed to hesitate, then commanded the soldiers to lower their weapons and answered the phone call.

His face changed slightly when he heard the first words, he said something in Uranian addressing Lukan and went aside. Lennart followed him with his eyes while Lukan and Frances looked at each other but no one spoke. Finally Jinescu returned.

"Must I stand here the whole morning?" asked Lennart suddenly. "It's awfully cold." The colonel didn't answer but looked at his prisoner with a very peculiar expression in his eyes.

"You know, Captain," he said after a long pause, "you truly were born under a lucky star. I intended to switch off my mobile this morning but forgot to do it. And I was just informed that your side agreed to our conditions. You will be deported tonight and brought to Dakstra, a Baron Confederation planet, where you will be delivered to the representatives of Deltan government. I hope you'll take into consideration the leniency which you have been shown over here. And for your own good, Captain, I hope that this will be our last meeting."

He turned and left. The line of soldiers broke. Lennart still couldn't fully comprehend the fact that he was free, but Lukan and Frances both came to congratulate him. They gave him a warm jacket, and brought him into the officers' canteen where he got a cup of coffee and a very decent breakfast.

A couple of hours later Lennart was standing in front of the mirror. He just finished shaving, he had taken a shower, and he was dressed in clean clothes which Lukan had provided him with. He and the major must have been originally of the same size but Lennart had lost so much weight lately that the clothes were hanging on him like on a coat hanger. Now without his beard and the rags he previously had to wear and with normal shoes on instead of combat boots, Lennart finally resembled a gentleman again. He looked at his own reflection in the mirror. He didn't seem to be changed much by the experience, only his eyes got a different expression.

Lennart asked Lukan for his address as he wanted to send him the money back, but the Uranian insisted that the clothes were meant as a present and positively refused to accept any compensation. "It's been an honor for me to get to know you, Captain," he stated and Lennart had to leave it at that.

During his two day trip to Dakstra he was treated quite well and chiefly spent his time thinking about his report, but the doctor had warned him that he would get a reaction, and he finally did when he came back to Delta. Lennart spent the next ten days in the hospital, with a new bout of pneumonia, suffering from heavy headaches and his left arm finally giving it up.

When he became somewhat better, he wrote his report and started thinking about his future. He had lost his business partner and his ship, and he frankly had no desire to start it all anew, now that Brian was gone. The money he inherited from him was barely enough to cover all Lennart's debts; moreover, he now became an invalid with but one arm. The doctor told him that unless a miracle happened he would never be able to use his left arm fully again. Thus he was unfit for military service as well.

Of course, he would get a pension from the government of Delta, but what would he do with himself? And then there was the question of

Eileen. Lennart knew that by now she had received his letter. His first impulse was to write her another one, but something stopped him. Would it not be better for her to think him dead and try and get a fresh start? What could he give her, in his present state?

He had no money, no job, and he was handicapped as well. Lennart was sure she would accept him, but the very idea of marrying her and using her late husband's money to start another business repulsed him. It was contrary to all his notions of honor and propriety. Lennart had always been a man of action, but now for the first time in his life he didn't know what to do.

He had seen Ferrash but once, briefly, when the latter came to visit him in the hospital, and since he submitted his report, he never heard anything from him. After two weeks, the doctor was finally satisfied with his progress and told Lennart he could leave the hospital whenever he wished to, which again created a problem. Lennart had no idea where he would go. During his previous visits to Delta he had always stayed with the Stewarts, which was now impossible for obvious reasons.

He had to rent a flat and started searching for one. The doctor lent him his laptop and Lennart, dressed up for the first time, sat on his bed perusing the advertisments when an orderly announced a visitor. "Colonel Ferrash to see you, Captain," he said and Ferrash went in.

"I'm glad to see you on your feet again, Major," he said and seeing Lennart's puzzled face expression he smiled and explained: "You were promoted to a higher rank. By the way, I read your report, Major, and also the report which Uranians sent us and I wanted to compliment you on your behavior."

"I was just doing my duty, nothing else," said Lennart simply but he had to turn away for a moment to conceal his emotion. "By the way, Colonel, I want to thank you for saving my life."

"There is someone else who you should thank as without his agreement you wouldn't have been exchanged," replied Ferrash to Lennart's great surprise. "You can do it now, if you wish to. He is waiting for us in the garden."

"OK", said Lennart.

He followed Ferrash through the corridor and into the hospital garden. The weather was nice, it was spring again and the flowers were blooming. There was a table with several chairs standing a little bit apart from others, and a man was sitting there, with his back towards the door, so that one couldn't see his face. It was an older man and his hair was gray. He looked slightly familiar to Lennart. The man heard them approaching, turned and stood up and with a shock Lennart recognized him.

"Lord Wallistan, here is your son," announced Ferrash. "I'd better leave you two alone as I think you have a lot to say to each other." He left. Lennart recovered from his initial shock and his face got its usual expression, cold and reserved. They stood and looked at each other and Lennart was the first to speak.

"So you have paid your debt, Father."

"Is this the only thing which you can say to me, Alex?" asked Lord Henry. "After all these years?"

"What else do you expect me to say?" inquired Lennart dryly.

"I guess I ought to tell you something," said the minister. "I should have told it to you long ago, but by some reason I didn't. I didn't kill your mother, Alex. I know that you hate me regardless, but may be you will hate me just a little bit less when you know this. And if you don't believe me you can ask Colonel Ferrash. He conducted his own private investigation of the matter and he will confirm that I'm telling the truth."

Lennart was silent for a moment, and his face stayed unmoved but when he spoke there was emotion in his voice, "Then who killed her?"

"It's a long story," sighed Lord Henry. "When your mother was young, she was a very beautiful girl, and she had a lot of admirers. One of them was a distant cousin of hers, whose name isn't important. She rejected him to marry me and he took it extremely ill, but after some time he finally left us alone. As years went by he got involved in politics and was on the other side of my party, always opposing me. When your mother died, believe it or not, it was a tremendous shock to me, and when I was consequently arrested for murder I was too stunned by the events to think logically, but when I was released I decided for myself that I would take action to find the murderer on my own. During that dreadful evening there were some extra servants hired for catering, and one of them had connections with that cousin. In short, I found him and he confessed his crime. He had been given a lot of money to place some powder into your mother's glass, which, he told me he had believed to be perfectly harmless. He had been told it was some sort of a prank, to make Lady Renata behave in a funny manner. The next day after our encounter he was killed by a car. I went to the cousin and confronted him, as I had all the evidence I needed. I gave him a choice and he chose to avoid scandal and shot himself. Thus your mother's death has been avenged."

Chapter 9. The Final One

After Lord Henry finished his story, there was a long silence. Lennart stood apparently deep in thought and his father waited for him to say something, but in vain. This time he was the first to break the silence.

"I want to officially acknowledge you as my son. You will get a passport with your own name on, your part of the inheritance and all the privileges which you deserve by birth, Alex."

"Aren't you afraid it will damage your career, sir?" asked Lennart. "People will be bound to know that you used your position as a minister to save me."

Lord Henry became visibly angry. "Just who do you think I am, Alex? I wouldn't lie to keep my job. After I had signed the order to release you, I went to the King and handed him my resignation and explained the reason for it, but he wouldn't accept it. You must think of me as some sort of a monster, but I'm quite capable of normal fatherly feelings. I didn't save you because I wanted to pay my debt, but because you are my son and I love you."

Lennart turned his face away. "And yet as far as I can remember you were only interested in Harry," he said stubbornly.

"One day, Alex, when you have children of your own, you will understand how much the firstborn son means to his father," answered the minister. "Goodness gracious, why are you so stubborn? Why can't you forgive and forget?"

"I did forgive you," replied Lennart and his voice trembled ever so slightly. "That night in prison when I was preparing to face the firing squad. Deep down I never believed you could have really killed my mother, that's why I had testified on your behalf. It's your affair which I could not forgive. Well, that night I looked back upon my life and realized I hardly had been a saint myself so I had no right to judge you. That's all."

"I made a mistake," admitted the minister, "and I have paid for it. I won't lie to you now and pretend that my second marriage was happy, but I won't speak ill of your stepmother, either. In fact, I would entreat you to forgive her, too, and pay her a visit. She's dying, Alex. The doctors give her no more than three months."

"I'm sorry to hear it, Father," said Lennart.

He turned his head and their eyes met, and at that moment Lennart's self-control broke and he couldn't conceal his tears, and neither could Lord

Henry. He embraced his son and so they stood for a moment, but then both drew back. They were very much like each other, as neither felt comfortable expressing his emotions. They sat together at the table and talked about all sorts of things, mostly Lennart was asking questions about old acquaintances and his brothers and their children.

"What are your plans now, Alex?" asked his father finally. "Ferrash probably had no time to tell you, but though you aren't fit for active service any more, there is an office job waiting for you by the military intelligence. I think you should accept it."

"Well, I guess I will," said Lennart. "As for my other plans, I can better tell you right away that I'm going to marry."

"Why, it's great news!" exclaimed Lord Henry. "I heard something about a girl called Margaret. Of course, she is below you in status but as she seems to be a sweet, innocent girl from a respected family, I will not object."

Lennart laughed. "So you heard this story, too, sir? I have forgotten how people gossip over here on Delta. I hate to disappoint you, Father, but it's not Margaret that I'm planning to marry. It's an Aarghean girl by the name of Eileen."

"Eileen who?" asked Lord Henry, whose face got visibly longer.

"Eileen D'haki Del Injra," replied Lennart. "She is a widow of a rich Volcani."

"You don't want to tell me, Alex, that you are going to marry someone from Volcan?" inquired his father.

"She comes from an upper class Aarghean family," explained Lennart, "but was kidnapped and sold into slavery. D'haki bought her and married her, and now she is a widow. Anyway, sir," he added, "I know that the law forbids a man to marry without his father's permission until he is thirty, but I'm not going to wait two more years. I either marry her as Lord Alex Nigel, your son, and bring her here, or as captain Lennart Duncan and live with her on Aargh, but marry her I will."

There was a long pause, but then Lord Henry finally spoke: "I guess after you lived all that time on your own, Alex, I have no right to interfere in your private affairs. You have my permission to marry. I only hope that your marriage will be happier than mine."

"Of this I'm sure, Father," said Lennart.

It took him some time to put his affairs in order, but finally three weeks later Lennart left for Volcan. There were things to arrange there and on Aargh as well since Drianon was going to be officially closed and Lennart had to pay back all his loans to the Aarghean bank. He accepted the position offered to him by Colonel Ferrash and decided that his future lay on Delta.

He rented an apartment in the capital, big enough for two people and planned to get married as soon as he came back. In the meanwhile, Lennart met his family and was warmly welcomed back by his brothers and their wives, and his nephews and nieces, half of whom were born after his disappearance.

He fullfilled his promise to his father and visited his stepmother, and when he saw how ill she looked he forgave her. She wanted to be present at his wedding, and he knew he had to hurry because her time in this world was running short. Lennart also wrote to Brendan Stewart and went on a short visit there, which was painful enough for all sides; and he spent an evening with Miss Nerts during which they had a long conversation and he thanked her for everything she had done for him.

It was strange to come to Volcan again, this time as a passenger. Lennart couldn't help remembering how he and Brian had left together three months ago and the pain of his loss came back to him again and for a moment he had to fight against tears, but he pulled himself together.

Lennart hired a taxi and gave the address, and after a short ride the car stopped in front of the familiar villa. A maidservant opened the door, looked at Lennart and started screaming. "Shut up, you idiot," said Lennart, but it was too late, as her screams attracted the attention of her mistress. Eileen came up to see what was going on.

She was dressed all in black, as usual, the black veil concealing her hair, and her face was pale and worn out with care. She looked up, saw Lennart and without saying a word sank to the floor, and he hardly had time to catch her.

"Will you ever forgive me, Eileen?" asked her Lennart half an hour later, when they were sitting together in the newly furnished living-room on a low sofa drinking coffee. "I have behaved like a pig and I know I don't deserve your affection, but I love you as I have never loved any woman in my life. All others didn't mean a thing. It's only after I met you that I realized what love truly is. Can I hope, Eileen?"

She looked at him and started crying, and through her tears saying "yes" and it took him some time to calm her down.

"You won't regret your decision," assured her Lennart. "I'm afraid I sinned against the Seventh Commandment but it's all in the past now. I will never give you a rival. The Deltan wedding vow speaks about forsaking all the others and I intend to keep it."

"Aminid wants me to become his fourth wife," said Eileen. "After he learned that both you and Brian were dead he became very insolent. He thinks he has the right to his brother's money, not some foreign ex-slave girl. You'll have a lot of problems with him."

"No, I won't," replied Lennart. "I would feel myself a scoundrel should I accept D'haki's money. I'm not a beggar and can provide for my family. Aminid may have everything."

"And your family on Delta?" asked the girl. "Are you sure they will accept me?"

"They can't wait to meet you," told her Lennart and it was true.

Aminid proved difficult to handle, because he wanted to have both the girl and the money, but he saw the shadow of Delta behind Lennart and had to agree to relinquish his claim, especially after he learned of Lennart's true position in society. He even helped Lennart to arrange the affair with the inheritance, and very warmly, but not entirely sincerely invited the young couple to come and visit him whenever they wished. Eileen cried when leaving the planet which had become her second home and asked Lennart to promise her to let her come back and visit her husband's grave and he agreed.

"It's a pity we can't do the same for poor Brian," she said.

"One day Tarna will be free and then we'll both go there," replied Lennart, and both were silent.

Lennart brought her to Delta and they had a quiet wedding ceremony, where the only people present besides the immediate family were Colonel Ferrash and Miss Nerts. A week after their wedding Lennart's stepmother died and then he had to go to Aargh to arrange the business matters there. Finally all his debts were paid and all his obligations to business partners fullfilled and he could come back.

Nearly a year had passed. Margaret got engaged to a young preacher. Her brother, who hadn't touched alcohol since the incident in Aranipor, moved to the North where he became a test pilot for a big company. Lennart's health improved against all the expectations, so that the doctor was surprised and announced it to be nothing short of a miracle. Eileen was eight months pregnant and Lennart knew that she was expecting twins, two boys, and he was tremendously proud.

That evening when he came home she was sitting in her favorite chair knitting something for the babies, her face serene and a faint smile upon her lips. It took Lennart some trouble to persuade her to get rid of black clothes and veils and start dressing according to Deltan fashions, in bright frocks and silly hats with flowers which he thought were very becoming to her.

Lennart went in and stood there looking at her, unable to say a word and Eileen who felt his gaze suddenly raised her head and was frightened by his face expression, she didn't know why.

"What is it, my lord?" she asked. "Did anything happen?"

"Not exactly," answered Lennart. "At least, not yet. Eileen, I'm terribly sorry, but I'm afraid I have to leave you. You see, my country needs a young energetic man like me with experience, or in other words I'm going to be deployed again and I'm not sure when I'm coming back."

She was silent, then asked in a low voice: "When do you have to leave?"

"Tomorrow morning," answered Lennart.

"It means we still have one night together."

"One night and the whole life," replied Lennart. "I will come back, I promise."

The next morning she was watching her husband pack his things.

"I love you," she said and Lennart smiled.

"I love you, too, more than anyone else in the world. Eileen, if I don't come back, I know I can trust you to raise my sons well."

He kissed her good-bye, went out and the door closed behind him.

www.ingramcontent.com/pod-product-compliance
Ingram Content Group UK Ltd.
Pitfield, Milton Keynes, MK11 3LW, UK
UKHW041944190726
13854UKWH00004B/1780

9 789081 961301